KINGS
of the
COURT

KINGS
of the
COURT

ALISON HUGHES

ORCA BOOK PUBLISHERS

Library and Archives Canada Cataloguing in Publication

Hughes, Alison, 1966–, author
Kings of the court / Alison Hughes.

Issued in print and electronic formats.
ISBN 978-1-4598-1219-2 (pbk.).—ISBN 978-1-4598-1220-8 (pdf).—
ISBN 978-1-4598-1221-5 (epub)

I. Title.
PS8615.U3165K56 2017   jC813'.6   C2016-904520-X
C2016-904521-8

First published in the United States, 2017
Library of Congress Control Number: 2016949053

Summary: In this humorous novel for middle-grade readers,
basketball-crazy Sameer tries to help the school team overcome
its aversion to a very dramatic new coach.

*Orca Book Publishers is dedicated to preserving the environment and
has printed this book on Forest Stewardship Council® certified paper.*

Orca Book Publishers gratefully acknowledges the support for its
publishing programs provided by the following agencies: the Government
of Canada through the Canada Book Fund and the Canada Council
for the Arts, and the Province of British Columbia through the
BC Arts Council and the Book Publishing Tax Credit.

Cover design by Jenn Playford
Cover photography by iStock.com and Dreamstime.com
Author photo by Barbara Heintzman

ORCA BOOK PUBLISHERS
www.orcabook.com

Printed and bound in Canada.

20 19 18 17 • 4 3 2 1

*For Chris, who painted the basketball
key on the backyard patio, and for everyone
who played backyard basketball at the
Burnham Avenue Court.*

ONE

Game Face

The noise in the gym was so loud, Sameer could feel it rumbling up through his chair and thrumming in his chest. It shook the scorers' table where he was sitting and jittered the pen beside the score sheet. The few adults in the gym had their hands over their ears, shaking their heads in alarm and giving each other pained smiles. Some kids in the crowd were doing the wave, and the non-waving sections were drumming their feet in a deafening frenzy on the bleachers as the seconds ticked down on the halftime break. Even during this pause in the basketball game, the Gladys Spinoza Junior High gym was a riot of cheering chaos.

Sameer smiled and pushed up his glasses. The atmosphere in the gym was exactly how he liked it. He swung his short legs happily, turned to Gracie and yelled, "Great crowd, eh?"

She shrugged. "The usual," she shouted back, smiling and shaking her head.

Sameer jumped as the buzzer sounded, scrambled off his chair and stood to high-five the team members as they ran back from their half-time shooting. Every guy on the team swung by the scorers' table to slap Sameer's hand.

"Great job, guys…Keep it up…Shots, shots, *shots*, Rochon…Nikho, they're playing close on D—burn around them and go to the hoop…You can take that number 3, *easy…Boards*, man, *boards*…You are getting *up* there, Nate! Whatcha been eating?…Hey, great support from the bench…" Sameer had a quick word of encouragement for every one of them.

"Sa*meer*!" Gracie tugged at his arm and pointed at the refs, who were at the center circle, looking impatient to start the half. Sameer and Gracie switched places at the table, and Gracie snatched up the pen and smoothed the score sheet. The scoring wasn't anywhere near as much fun as the announcing, so he and Gracie had agreed to call one half, score the next. Sameer adjusted the microphone and pulled a paper with cryptic stats on it from his pocket. Then he settled his elbows on the table, put his chin on his fists, closed his eyes and savored the moment.

Gracie had done a great job calling the first half. She had a knack for description, a quick, lively delivery and great give-and-take with the crowd. It was a tough act to follow. Sameer took a deep breath, reminded himself how much he loved basketball and this team, opened his eyes and flicked on the mic.

"We're *back*, you pounding maniacs!" he thundered. The crowd roared its approval. "You guys are *amazing*! No school has spirit like Gladys Spinoza school spirit! We are most definitely in *GLADIATOR* COUNTRY!" Sameer's friend Vijay, the Gladiators' mascot, brandished a silver garbage-can-lid "shield" and dollar-store sword in a menacing and bloodthirsty manner, racing back and forth and baying at the appreciative crowd.

Gracie elbowed Sameer and pointed to the players on the court, her eyebrows raised.

"Whoops," Sameer said into the mic, "you guys are such a great crowd that I almost forgot I'm supposed to call this thing! Thanks, Gracie. Okay, well, the Bobcats blew that shot, so we haven't missed any scoring. It's 42–39 at the half, and the Gladiators are close, so *close*, to their first win of the whole season, after losing—well, after losing a *lot*!"

From the sidelines on his left, Coach Bosetti threw Sameer a dirty look. Coach Boss had his game face on, and it wasn't pretty. He was packed tightly into a gray Gladiators sweatshirt, and he looked, as usual, red-faced and angry. He paced the sidelines, swinging his clipboard and bellowing at his team.

"Boards! *Boards*! Do you understand? BOARDS! REBOUND! Speak English? You guys are PATHETIC!"

Sameer ignored him. "Bobcats sit at second-to-last place in the league, so Gladiators, this may be our game!"

"Block out! BLOCK. OUT. NATE! WHAT ARE YOU *DOING*?" Coach Boss's scream ripped through the gym, louder than Sameer with the mic. Nate, a sensitive, awkward redhead, glanced nervously over at Coach Boss, then flushed and skittered into the key like a young giraffe, one of his long legs accidentally tripping a player from the other team who was driving in for a layup. The ref blew a short blast on the whistle. Nate had the misfortune of already being six foot five and not entirely in control of his arms and legs.

"Foul on number 12, Nathan Schneider," Sameer said quietly into the mic. He glanced down at the score sheet and added quickly, "*But* that's only Big Nate's second foul, folks, which is really excellent for a big man in a tight game. He's been putting up monster rebounds this game too."

"Sub! SUB!" roared Coach Boss.

As Nate came back to the bench, his face white and anxious, Sameer gave him a thumbs-up and a quick, closed-eyes headshake that meant "Shake it off, buddy—don't let him get you down."

"Substitution. Number 16, Kenneth Otombo, coming in for Nate. He may be their spark off the bench," Sameer reported to the crowd. "This is Kenneth's first appearance this game, so let's give him a big Gladiator salute!"

The people in the crowd jumped to their feet, raised their fists above their heads and roared, "Charge!"

"Yeah, that's what I'm talking about!" Sameer grinned and stood, raising his fists along with the crowd.

Play continued, and the Gladiators' best shooter, Rochon, started to get hot.

"Rochon, the Rockin' Roch-Man, *raining* down threes! Burying them! Shooting the lights out!" Sameer whipped the crowd into a frenzy, "Shooting three for seven from downtown! Better outside shooting percentage than *Kobe Bryant* last night! We'll take it! Oh yes, we'll take that three, thank you very much! Oh, wait, what's this? The Bobcats' coach has just wisely called a time-out. Yes, sir, smart plan." Sameer nodded at the other coach, who ignored him. "He's gotta stop the bleeding! Because these Gladiators, *your* Gladiators, are on *fire*!" The crowd cheered as both teams jogged in to their benches.

"Great job, guys!" he called after flicking off the mic. Blaring music filled the gym, and the cheer team ran in to execute a complicated routine.

Vijay ran over to Sameer and Gracie. His helmet wobbled perilously as he ran. "Hi, guys," he said, looking only at Gracie.

"Your helmet's crooked there, tough guy." Gracie laughed and turned away to talk to a friend.

Vijay dumped his sword and shield on the ground and pulled off his gladiator helmet. Sameer and Vijay had spent a whole evening making it, covering an old bike helmet in duct tape and tinfoil and glue-gunning a yellow sponge-mop head along the top. Vijay reached behind Sameer and grabbed Sameer's hoodie to wipe his sweaty face.

"Okay, that's *disgusting*," protested Sameer, looking up from studying the score sheet. He snatched his hoodie back.

Vijay grinned, showing gums and a line of big front teeth. "Hot in this thing. Like, *hot* hot." He gestured down at the peeling silver tunic someone had donated from an old Halloween knight's costume. He was wearing it over his regular gym clothes.

"Speaking of your gladiator costume, Vijay," Sameer said, "couldn't you maybe wear black shorts and a black shirt? Or red? I mean, team colors are black and red. Those green shorts, that yellow shirt…" He shook his head dismissively. "Unprofessional. Plus, they stink. Just saying."

"Yeah yeah, whatever." Vijay wasn't listening. "So, Sameer," he said, his eyes snaking sideways to look at Gracie, "has she mentioned me? Like, at all? In any way?"

"Oh yeah, Vijay. You're all we've been talking about," said Sameer sarcastically. "It's just been 'Vijay' this and 'Vijay' that! Look, we're in the middle of a basketball game, if you haven't noticed. I'm *working*, okay?"

"I'm working too," said Vijay, leaning in annoyingly close and breathing in Sameer's ear. "Working on loooove."

"*Go*," said Sameer, batting him away.

Vijay grinned, then jumped as Coach Boss's clipboard hit the wall behind him.

"*Man*, he's throwing things now?" Vijay looked over his shoulder with alarm at the huddled Gladiators and the huge, ranting man. "I mean, not just screaming like usual? Wait, aren't we winning?" Vijay checked the scoreboard, even though Sameer was nodding. "Yeah, we're winning. Rochon was raining them in there."

Sameer shook his head. "He's a terrible coach. No clue how to motivate players, how to use their strengths. Just rant and rave, shame and blame. Only ever plays five, maybe six guys, even if they're dog-tired, like *now*. And look at the talent we have on the bench—" Sameer was interrupted by the whistle ending the time-out.

"Go, Vijay. Shoo."

Vijay had already turned to Gracie.

"Guess I gotta get back to my fans," he said, grinning at Gracie and her friend Simone. He put his hand to his ear. "Hear that? The crowd's calling me. Calling their number one Gladiator. Got to… gladiate." He picked up his sword and shield, shoved on his helmet, gave a corny salute and ran off to lead the crowd in the GLAD-I-A-TORS cheer. Each of the four sections of the bleachers had a syllable, and Vijay conducted them like a maniac, running up and down, first slowly, then with increasing speed, until it all broke loose into laughter and applause and foot stomping.

"Such a goof," said Simone.

"Sort of cute though," said Gracie. "In a way."

Sameer pushed up his glasses and looked over at Gracie. *Seriously? Vijay?*

"If you like skinny little brown guys," blurted Sameer, looking down and pretending to study his notes. Where did that come from? he thought. Vijay is my friend…

"*You're* a little brown guy." Gracie laughed, swatting Sameer on the shoulder with the back of her hand.

"An even *littler* brown guy," Simone pointed out. "Not so skinny though…"

"Okay, okay, Simone. You can stop right there." Sameer's ears felt hot.

Simone looked at him, her head tilted and her eyes narrowed.

"Hmmm. Maybe Vijay's not the only one who likes—"

"Oh, look," Sameer interrupted in desperation, pointing urgently at the court, "here's a *basketball game* that's happening in this gym. And here's a *mic*! Maybe I better call this thing."

"Yep, back to work. Go, Simone." Gracie shooed her friend away.

"Aaand we're back, Gladiator Nation!" said Sameer into the mic. "Anybody else find that the longest time-out *ever*? Let's play some ball!"

TWO

Eee-jected!

I t was a long fourth quarter. The constant, belligerent pressure from Coach Boss had the Gladiators rattled and racking up some cheap fouls.

"Unbelievable," Sameer said into the mic, shaking his head. "Foul on number 22, Kyle Runningbear. This game is getting out of hand! Guys who *never* hack are getting called. Even Quiet Kyle gets a foul! Incidentally, Kyle blocked that shot, so it may have been worth the foul, and he's been a *wall* on defense all night. We've still got plenty of basketball, folks, but the refs are calling this game incredibly close. The tension is palpable."

Sameer wasn't actually sure what *palpable* meant, but he'd heard the NBA announcers use it the night before. Gracie would have elbowed him if it had been wrong. Like last game, when he'd used *fracas* as a verb: *One thing this team does is fracas well.* He'd thought it sounded very smooth, even impressive, but Gracie had grabbed his arm and hissed at him that *fracas* meant "a noisy brawl." Without missing a beat, he had continued, *Yes, indeed, this game has been a complete fracas.*

At every foul, Vijay started up a cheer where half the gym shouted, "HACK!" and the other shouted, "ATTACK!" Pointless, thought Sameer, but Vijay really does have a knack for keeping the crowd involved in the game.

Coach Boss, never one to take the high road in stressful situations, was screaming louder than ever at his players. "Engage brain! ENGAGE BRAIN!"

More ominously, he had been arguing calls with the refs all game. He was arguing Kyle's foul right now.

"Are you freakin' kiddin' me? Are you JOKING?" he yelled at one of the refs. "He was straight up!" Coach Boss raised both hands over his head, pushing out his big gut. "Straight up! You're out of your mind!"

Keep it up, Coach Boss, and you're out of this game, Sameer thought, just as the ref made a T sign with his hands. And here we go...

"Coach Bosetti teed up. Technical foul," Sameer explained to the crowd. He hesitated, glanced over at Coach Boss, who was arguing the call with the ref, then quickly added, "Interestingly, Coach Boss is averaging 1.5 technical fouls a game so far this season."

Coach Boss turned and roared, "Shut *up*, Sameer!"

Sameer didn't dignify that with even a glance. He flicked off the mic and turned to Gracie. "Wow, crazy game, hey?"

"Ug-u-ly." She nodded, twirling her pen.

"Does Coach Boss ever think about how unprofessional he looks?"

"I don't think he cares. About anything," said Gracie, her sunny face unusually serious. "He's such a jerk it's *embarrassing*. I mean, *look* at him."

Sameer looked over to see Coach Boss fling his clipboard into the corner of the gym and then growl at Anil, a forward who was having an off game, pushing his finger into the player's chest for emphasis.

"Oh, *man*. I can feel this game slipping away. Time check, Gracie?"

"About two minutes left," she said.

Sameer nodded and clicked on the mic.

"Another point for the Bobcats for the technical foul. Number 6 has shot a perfect five for five from the charity stripe." He paused, then continued in a loud, enthusiastic voice. "Okay, Gladiator Nation, you have two minutes to help your Gladiators get back on track! It ain't over till it's over! Time to make some noise!"

The crowd didn't need much encouragement to go wild. Vijay scrambled to pull a huge cardboard letter *D* and a piece of white plastic fencing from a garbage bag in preparation for the D-Fence cheer.

Coach Boss argued on the possession of a ball that went out, then picked up the ball, which had rolled near the bench, and fired it back at the ref. The ref dodged it—and gave him another technical.

"Coach, you're out of this gym. Now." The ref made a dramatic, unmistakable thumb-over-the-shoulder motion.

"I was passing you the ball!" said Coach Boss with unconvincing astonishment. "It was a *pass*." He slumped his shoulders and spread his big hands wide as if bewildered and frustrated.

"Sameer!" Gracie said above the excited babble of the crowd, "Coach Boss just got *kicked out*!"

Sameer smiled and nodded. "Eee-jected! Make no mistake, sports fans," he said into the mic, "this is a tense game! Coach Boss is outta here, tossed, heading for the change rooms! The score is 53–51 for the Bobcats. But the Gladiators are pounding on the door!"

To the crowd's delight, Vijay ran over to the gym door and thrashed away at it with his fake sword until Coach Boss shoved him aside to stomp out of the gym. Sameer saw Mrs. Lee, the school's principal, who was sitting at the front of the bleachers, watching Coach Boss, her face set and angry.

Sameer was busy thinking. There was no other coach because both assistant coaches, nice university guys looking to do some volunteer work with their old school team, had quit weeks ago in protest against Coach Boss's tactics. They had to have a coach to continue—league rule 3(3)(a). Otherwise, if they *did* win, the other team could contest the win. Sameer made a quick decision.

"Vijay, come to the scorers' table, please," he said into the mic. "Vijay, scorers' table now, please."

Vijay swung around and ran over, a question in his eyes. "What's up, Sameer? Hey, did you see Coach Boss's face? Completely *purple*—"

"No time, Vijay." Sameer stood up. "Can you score for the last couple of minutes? Gracie, can you take over calling the rest of the game?"

"Sure," she said, slipping into Sameer's chair. Vijay scuttled behind the scorers' table. His sword and shield clattered to the ground.

"Uh, I'm not too sure…" Vijay said, looking down at the score sheet, vaguely waving the pen above it.

"Look, just don't write anything or touch anything until I tell you to, okay?" Gracie said to Vijay, her hand over the mic.

"Gotcha!" Vijay snatched off his wobbly helmet, scraped his chair closer to Gracie and winked at Sameer.

Sameer picked up the clipboard that Coach Boss had thrown into the corner and walked over to the Gladiators, who were standing uncertainly in a circle. The guys on the bench were hunched over, quiet and nervous. Rabbit nervous. The starters weren't so quiet.

"Sameer! Man, what's *happening*..."

"He's going to be so mad, Sameer, soooo mad..."

"Did you see Boss's face, Sameer? We're gonna run suicides for the next *week*..."

"Goes and gets himself kicked out! Nice! Great! Like we need another technical. We're already down by two points."

The crowd had started to pound on the bleachers to jinx the Bobcat player's shot from the free-throw line. Sameer shook his head at this unsportsmanlike behavior. The Bobcat made the shot anyway.

"Oh, *man*," Rochon said. "Three. We're down by three now."

The whistle blew. The team tensed up.

"Forget it. We have two minutes," said Sameer calmly. "Two minutes is a lifetime in basketball.

Calm down, run the plays, solid D, and let's actually have some fun out there. Oh, and while you're having fun, get the ball to Rochon. Rochon, green light—you're shooting every single time you touch the ball, right?" Rochon nodded.

"Hands in," Sameer said. "Team on three?"

"One, two, three, TEAM!" They ran back out, and Sameer wiped away the trickle of sweat snaking down the side of his face. Oh please, oh please, he thought, perching on the edge of the bench.

"Sameer," said one of the twins, either Hassan or Mohammed, reaching a long arm over the other twin to nudge Sameer's leg. He pointed down the bench, to where the principal was taking a seat at the end. Mrs. Lee waved as they both looked over at her.

"Just being the token adult, Coach," she called, and Sameer grinned.

"We're back!" announced Gracie. "What a gong show this game has been! But it all comes down to these crucial last couple of minutes."

The Bobcats inbounded and charged, their quick guard slipping in for a layup. From across the key, Nate lunged desperately, his long arm blocking the shot.

"DE-NIED!" Gracie cried into the mic. "*Monster* block from big Nate!"

Nikho scrambled for the ball and flipped it to Kyle, under the basket. Kyle put it up and got fouled.

"Best guy to have on the foul line," Sameer babbled nervously to nobody in particular. He pushed up his glasses. "A 72 percent free-throw shooter. Reliable. Calm guy." He dug his nails into his palms.

Kyle sank the first shot, but the second rolled around the rim and flipped out. Nate got the rebound, looked around wildly, saw Tom, who swung it around fast to Rochon, hovering just outside the three-point line.

The crowd bellowed a countdown of the dwindling seconds of the game.

"FIVE! FOUR! THREE!"

He has to shoot, he has to shoot…

"Shoot!" Sameer croaked feebly from the bench.

Rochon shrugged off his man and got open.

"TWO! ONE!" the crowd chanted.

He shot.

"Shot's up! A buzzer beater!" announced Gracie. "Aaand…"

Sameer, on his feet like the rest of the bench, the rest of the gym, watched the ball arc toward the basket as if it were in slow motion. It clanged on the rim as the end-of-game buzzer sounded. Short.

"Nope, no basket. That's gotta hurt," said Gracie sadly to a suddenly quiet gym.

Rochon bent over, his head in his hands.

Sameer rushed onto the court and slipped an arm around Rochon's shoulders, trying to think of something to say. Rochon knew it was a team loss, not just one missed shot. Loads of clichés ran through Sameer's mind—the game was a heart-breaker, a nail-biter, a knock-out punch, a back-breaker, it went down to the wire—but nothing Rochon would want to hear.

There was nothing to say.

The Gladiators were in last place. Again. Still.

But we're not losers, thought Sameer, looking around at his friends' long faces. We may have lost this game, but we're not losers.

"Everybody in!" he called. He slapped each player's hand as the team walked back to the bench.

They looked up at Sameer.

"Yeah, it sucks," he admitted. "But that game's over. Done. We gave them a great fight, and we move on."

Mrs. Lee came over. "Tough loss, boys. Good effort. Now, everybody grab some chairs and help clear this gym."

The team silently stacked chairs as the crowd drained out of the gym.

THREE
Dig Deep

Later that evening, Sameer sat slumped on the basement couch, watching an NBA game. His father came down during the third quarter.

"Good game?" he asked, pointing at the television.

"Nah. Bit of a blowout."

"Huh." They watched in silence. "So the blue are the—"

"Knicks. Celtics are in white. Knicks are up by seventeen," Sameer added, because his father was sure to ask even though the score was right there in the bottom left corner.

His father cleared his throat.

"Your nani would've appreciated you watching her beloved Celtics. Even if they're getting hammered."

"Yeah," Sameer agreed, his eyes stinging with tears. He had just been thinking about how much he missed his grandmother. He would never watch a Celtics game without thinking about her. She had been a fellow fan, his basketball buddy who never missed a game. She had been, if anything, the more rabid fan, the one yelling up the stairs that the game had started, telling him that his homework could wait, genuinely appreciating the stats he relayed, making each game an event.

Her strong opinions had lasted right up until she died.

"*What a BUM!*" she would shout in disgust when her raspy voice was still strong. "*Are they BRIBING these refs now?*" She would scream, "*DUNK! That's what I'm talking about! Look at the airtime that guy gets!*" They would seriously debate the merits of a trade, a player's stats or a team's chances for the playoffs. And often she would press *Mute* and say, "*Okay, Sami, your turn.*

Make it good!" and he would commentate the game while she cackle-laughed in appreciation.

Even in her last days, a few months ago, she would shuffle slowly out of her suite in their basement to the TV room and watch the games with him, her tiny, failing body muffled up in her Celtics fleece blanket. Then, when walking became too much for her, Sameer's mom bought a TV for his grandmother's room, anchoring it to the wall so Nani could watch from her bed. Sameer would lie beside her, watching the game while she dozed on and off. And even then, even that last night, she'd surprised him. He'd thought his grandmother was asleep, but she hadn't been.

"Foul," she'd whispered, feebly raising a hand to point at the game. *"Sami, that was a foul if I've ever seen one."*

"I'll always watch the Celtics, Dad," Sameer said now. "For Nani." The tears threatened again, and he blinked them away. *"Somebody's* got to scream at them."

His father laughed, slapping Sameer's knee.

"Spurs are still your team though. She wouldn't want you to cheer for a team that wasn't yours."

That was true. Sameer remembered her saying, "*Stick with your team. Thick and thin. Be a true fan.*" Fiercely loyal to her Celtics to the end.

Sameer and his father watched in silence.

"Bad day at school?" his father ventured, glancing over at Sameer.

"Just…basketball. Gladiators lost again."

"Did you commentate the game?"

"Yeah, with Gracie Kim. That part of it was great. Game sucked though. Lost by two."

"Ah, well."

"We're in last place. Dead last."

"It happens," his father said philosophically. "It's just junior-high ball, right?" He had his eyes on the game and missed Sameer's sad smile.

His grandmother would have understood how much it meant. They would have dissected the whole game. She would have questioned him, argued with him, listened to him analyze how each player performed, how Coach Boss behaved, how the team could improve. She would have said things like, "So hotshot Rochon isn't quite as clutch as he thinks," or "I like the sound of that Kyle. Good fundamentals," or "But how was Nikho's passing? That's the measure of a point guard." No detail was too small for someone who loved the game.

"Anyway," his father mused, "it's not like it's *you* getting blown out game after game. Feel like you had a bit of a lucky escape?"

Sameer was silent. He'd never questioned Coach Boss's decisions about who made (and didn't make) the team. The right guys had made it. Sameer knew he was short and slow and not very skilled, but he'd hoped and prayed that playing intelligently and working hard might make up for his drawbacks. But it still hurt. It hurt that the thing he loved to do was not the thing he happened to be very good at. No, given the chance, even losing game after game, he would wear the Gladiators jersey in a heartbeat.

His grandmother had sat down on the couch beside Sameer after she'd found out he hadn't made the team. They'd watched the Raptors play Cleveland in complete silence.

As the seconds drained away in the fourth quarter, she'd said, "*Sameer, in basketball, as in life, there are many ways to contribute. And you have a lot to contribute. Find your place. And when you've found it, dig in, and dig deep."*

Sameer's mom came down the stairs now and settled in a chair. His parents had been making an effort to come down and watch some of the games with him since Nani died. Sameer appreciated this, but it wasn't the same.

"Ah, another basketball game. Wow, these things are on every night!" His mother darted a glance at Sameer, then at his father.

They watched in silence for a minute before his mom asked, "So who's the blue team again?"

FOUR
Die-Hard Fans

"Freezing in here," Vijay complained for the fourth time, looking miserably around the rickety team bus. All the Gladiators were there, silent, shivering, huddled into their seats.

"If you would wear a proper coat…" murmured Sameer, not looking up from his stats book.

"Like yours?" Vijay looked dismissively at Sameer's black downfill. "No thanks. You look like a marshmallow. A *burnt* marshmallow."

"Oh, you're right, Vijay, *much* better to be shivering in that stupid thin leather coat. Very cool."

"Mmm-hmm. At least I'm not marshmallow man." Vijay slapped his thighs. "*Man*, what's with this bus? It's warmer *outside*! You'd think it would at least block the wind." Vijay held up a thin hand to the window. "Wind," he said darkly, "comin' right in here. What a piece of junk."

"It's about a hundred years old," said Sameer. "Falling apart. Doesn't help that Coach Boss drives it like a maniac off-roader."

Anil turned around from the seat in front of them. "He climbed right up a curb last time we played McGee. Rattled right up onto the sidewalk practically to the front door. We looked like a bunch of idiots."

Sameer shook his head.

"Hey, at least it's a ride to the south side, I guess," said Vijay, huddling in closer to Sameer.

The bus was quiet. Nobody was looking forward to playing Alexander McGee, the team that always, year after year, held first place in their league's standings. Many of them were actively dreading it. It was always a loss; it was only a question of how dismal a loss it would be.

"Finally. Here he comes," said Vijay.

Coach Boss lumbered over to the bus, wearing his old high-school football jacket that didn't come anywhere near to closing in the front anymore.

Why does he always look angry? Sameer wondered, looking up from his stats. What could possibly make a person mad all the time? Not just when things get frustrating, but always? I mean, he's got some weight issues, and yeah, some hair issues, but really? Does that have to make him insanely angry all the time?

The bus groaned and lurched to the side as Coach Boss thumped up the steps and sank into the driver's seat.

"Everybody here?" he barked, looking in the rearview mirror. His small eyes sharpened. "Hey, you two! Sameer, Vijay! Out!"

"Just thought we could catch a ride to the game. Sir," said Vijay, smiling his gummy, ingratiating smile.

"Nope. New policy. Team bus only. Out!"

Sameer strongly suspected that the new policy might have something to do with his helping out in the last game. Coach Boss had watched the last two minutes with narrowed eyes from the small window in the gym door.

"But we've always—"

"Out!"

"Look. Coach Boss," Sameer said in a calm voice, "it'll take us three buses to get even remotely near to McGee. We'd miss half the game."

"Plus it's, like, minus fifty out there," pleaded Vijay. "Like, *cold* cold."

"There's just two of them, Coach, there's room," said Kenneth from the back of the bus.

"Yeah," murmured a few of the other guys.

"There's *no* room!"

"But what about this seat we're actually sitting on?" Vijay said, following Sameer's lead of good-natured reasonableness. "*That's* room."

"Out!" Coach Boss started the bus and revved the engine hard. "Out! NOW!" he bellowed.

It was hopeless. "C'mon, Vijay," muttered Sameer.

"Many coaches would treat their team's die-hard fans with a little respect," Sameer said as they walked up the aisle to the bus doors.

"Sorry, guys," Nate said quietly as they passed.

"Forget it, Nate," Sameer whispered. "Hey, use those freakishly long arms on defense today, okay?"

Nate smiled and nodded.

Coach Boss slammed the door shut behind them, and the bus peeled out of the school parking lot, creaking and rattling around the corner.

"Jerk," said Vijay, shivering and shoving his hands in his pockets. "Oh well, we tried, hey?"

"What do you mean?" Sameer said blankly.

"We *tried* to go to the game," Vijay said. "What more can we do? It's not like we're going to ride the bus for an hour and a half to get to the game on the south side…" He saw Sameer's face. "Oh, come on, Sameer. You're joking. Seriously? It's so cold." He blew into his fists.

Sameer was studying a bus schedule he'd pulled out of his backpack.

"Vijay, any fan can go to a game when it's in their own gym. Just stroll on down the hallway when they have nothing better to do. Anybody can do that. But die-hard fans show up even when it involves hardship."

"Oh, *man*," Vijay whimpered, stamping his feet.

"Hardship and sacrifice. You coming or staying?"

"Shut up."

"Because you don't have to come." Sameer started walking.

"I hate you," Vijay said as he trailed after Sameer.

"So if we catch the 53 it should get us to Westgate shopping center, then from there…well, we'll figure it out."

They waited at the bus stop in silence. Vijay hunched against the wind, his back to Sameer.

A van pulled out of the school parking lot and slowed as it passed them. Gracie leaned out the window.

"Hey, Sameer! Vijay! You guys need a ride?"

"Absolu—" started Vijay excitedly, but Sameer cut him off.

"Nah, it's okay, Gracie, thanks. We're going to the game at McGee. All the way on the south side."

"That's where we're going! To McGee. Other gym is the girls' game. Got a bunch of the girls' team here because nobody'll ride on the team bus anymore. But we got two vans, so there's room. The guys'll need some fans. It'll be a slaughter."

"Please, please, *please*." Vijay turned to Sameer.

"Great, thanks, Gracie. Thanks, Mrs. Kim," Sameer said as he followed Vijay into the warm van.

"Thanks, ladies," said Vijay, smiling. "I was freezing! Like, *freezing* freezing." He let Sameer have the window and squeezed in between him and another girl. "But, you know, you do it because you're a Gladiator, right? A die-hard fan."

"You're a big hero, Vijay," said Simone from the back of the van, rolling her eyes.

Vijay ignored her. He smiled at Gracie in the front seat, leaned forward and held out his hands to the warm air pumping from the heat vent.

"Yep, hardship and sacrifice, my friend," Vijay said softly, grinning at Sameer. "Hardship and sacrifice..."

FIVE
Huddle Up

"Mrs. Jackson, could you send Sameer down to the office, please? Mrs. Lee wants to speak to him." The school secretary's voice crackled over the class intercom.

The announcement energized the slumped students in the eighth-grade Language Arts class, whose interest in a short story had been flagging for a while. They sat up.

"Oohhhhhhhhh!" They all made the loud, mandatory sound for when a classmate got called to see the principal.

"What did you do now, Sameer?"

"You're in trouble!"

"Suspended?"

"Expelled?"

"Okay, okay, you're all very funny," Mrs. Jackson said wearily. "Sameer, are you finished the short story?"

"Yep," said Sameer, who had finished reading the story and also written the essay on it, which wasn't due for a month. Not a big fan of Language Arts, he liked to get his least-favorite things out of the way early.

"Sandy," Mrs. Jackson called in the direction of the speaker, "he'll be right down."

Sameer shut *Buzzer Beaters and Hail Marys: A Hundred Years of Professional Sports Jargon, Slang and Lingo,* which he'd been reading furtively behind his textbook, and shoved it into his backpack.

He walked down the empty halls to the office, feeling uneasy. He didn't think he was in trouble, and he certainly wasn't getting suspended or expelled, but he wondered what Mrs. Lee could possibly want to see him about. Marks? He was at the top of the class in everything except Language Arts, and even there he did pretty well. He wasn't much of a reader of anything other than sports trivia and stats books—he couldn't see the point of making up stories or, worse, writing about stories other people made up. This short story they were reading, for example. It was about wallpaper. Yellow wallpaper. What on earth was the point of that?

Anyway, it couldn't be about marks. What else were principals interested in? Absences? Nothing there. Lateness? Nope. He was always early. School property? He paused uneasily, wondering if Vijay had damaged or destroyed something important in a Gladiator-mascot frenzy. Sameer remembered Vijay thrashing at the gym door with his fake sword. And then he thought of the previous night's game.

The secretary glanced up when he entered the office.

"Hi, I'm Sameer," he said. "Mrs. Lee wanted to see me?"

She nodded and returned to typing at her computer. "Just go on back. They're waiting for you."

They? Who were *they*?

Sameer smoothed a hand over his thatch of thick black hair.

Down the hallway and to the left, the principal's office door stood open. Vijay was sitting at a table, looking small and nervous. A big redheaded woman sat across from him. Her face and neck were blotchy, and her eyes were red and puffy. She gave him a watery smile.

Wait…that's Big Nate's mom, thought Sameer.

"Ah. Sameer. Good," Mrs. Lee said. "Take a seat." She got up and motioned him over to the table they were sitting at. Then she closed the office door.

Sameer sat on the edge of the chair and pushed up his glasses.

"So. Sameer. Vijay. The basketball game. Yesterday. At McGee. You were there?" Mrs. Lee shot this at them with her trademark rapid-fire delivery.

They both nodded. Vijay swallowed nervously, his prominent Adam's apple bobbing up and down.

"Yes, ma'am," he added.

Suck-up, thought Sameer.

"Well? How did it go?" Mrs. Lee was staring at them intently through her heavy glasses. It was like being under a microscope.

Sameer and Vijay looked at each other. It had been a massacre. A disaster. A complete mess. Who was going to say that?

"Well," said Sameer slowly, "we lost. Badly. You want the score or—"

"No, no," said Mrs. Lee sharply. "I know we lost. Doesn't matter." She looked over at the blotchy woman. "Mrs. Schneider says Nathan told her that Coach Bosetti was out of control."

"*Crazy*. A crazy man!" Nate's mom gulped, throwing her big hands in the air. "Nate said he was mean—mean*er* than usual."

Vijay pointed at Nate's mom approvingly. "That's it. You got it. Mean*er*. Crazi*er*. Scream*ier*." He looked at Mrs. Lee with satisfaction, nodding as though he'd just explained everything. Mrs. Lee stared at him, then adjusted her chair so she was facing Sameer.

"Sameer, I need your help. Explain what happened, please."

Sameer shifted uncomfortably. "Maybe you should talk to some of the guys on the team," he said.

"Oh, I have. There seems to be a general reluctance to talk."

Sameer could understand this. They had to deal with Coach Boss every day at practice.

"Now I'm asking you," Mrs. Lee said. "An impartial fan."

"So this is strictly confidential, right?" Sameer asked.

"Yeah, no way at all this is getting back to Coach Boss?" Vijay asked. He had Coach Boss for phys ed this semester.

Mrs. Lee nodded. "Absolutely private. Between us. I just want the truth."

"Okay, look, I don't know why—personal issues, whatever—but Coach Boss seems to be increasingly out of control lately," Sameer said.

"Mean*er*," offered Vijay. Mrs. Lee held up a hand in his direction without looking at him. Sameer continued.

"But last night he was *completely* out of control. Absolutely. More so than usual. They were getting hammered. Hey, it's McGee, right? Nobody beats them—nobody *expects* to beat them…"

Mrs. Lee made an impatient gesture. "Yes, yes. Coach Bosetti. What did he do?"

"The usual. Yelling. Screaming. Throwing his clipboard."

"And?"

"He got a couple of technicals. Again."

"Ejected from the game?" asked Mrs. Lee.

"Oh yeah," Sameer said, remembering the menacing, lumbering figure walking straight across the court and crashing open both gym doors.

"Why?" Mrs. Lee shot at him.

"First technical was for screaming at the referee, which is nothing new. Second technical was for unsportsmanlike conduct." Sameer glanced at Nate's mom. "Against his own team."

"What exactly did he do, Sameer?"

"He fired a ball at Nate's head."

"There you go," said Nate's mom to Mrs. Lee, throwing out her arm and sitting back in her chair.

"Hit him right smack in the nose!" said Vijay, relaxed now and happy to pile on. "We thought it was *broken*, because of all the blood. Turns out it wasn't. Sameer and I ran and got, like, *thousands* of paper towels from the washroom. Took a whole stack to mop it all up. Pretty gross."

"It couldn't have been accidental? He wasn't, for example, passing him the ball?" Mrs. Lee asked.

Sameer cleared his throat. "Uh, pretty sure not. He really wound up before the throw. And he screamed, '*You ginger MORON!*' when he threw it."

Vijay stifled a giggle. "I didn't hear that," he said to Sameer. Then he looked nervously at Mrs. Lee and Mrs. Schneider. "*Very* inappropriate."

"To be honest, I think he aimed for the back of Nate's head, but Nate sort of swung around and got it in the face. Sorry, Mrs. Schneider," said Sameer. "I'm sure you don't want to hear this. I'm just trying to be accurate."

"No, no, Shaheer. I'm very grateful to you," Nate's mom said.

"Anyway," Sameer said to Mrs. Lee, "that's how it went."

"It's mean and insulting! That's what it is! *Bullying*! It's probably even *criminal*," said Mrs. Schneider in a wobbly voice. "Nate didn't want me to come here. I knew he hadn't been exactly enjoying basketball, but you know when

46

your child, your *child*, comes home from a game with a bloody nose and two black eyes, you have to *do* something."

"Absolutely. Absolutely," Mrs. Lee said, tapping one finger on the table. She looked very serious, her eyes narrowed. Mrs. Lee was tiny, even shorter than Sameer himself, but she was tough. Watching her face, Sameer felt a pang of something like pity for Coach Boss, who was probably, at this minute, blithely bullying somebody else or ineptly teaching some cowed class, unaware of what was coming.

"Thank you, Sameer. Vijay. That's it, I hope," said Mrs. Lee.

Vijay scrambled to his feet.

"Um, one last thing," said Sameer, tentatively holding up his index finger. "I guess you should probably know that Coach Boss drove off in the bus before the end of the game."

"*What?*" Mrs. Lee and Mrs. Schneider spoke at the same time.

"Nate didn't tell me that," said Mrs. Schneider, shocked.

"It worked out okay though," Sameer said quickly. "Some of the guys caught rides back with the girls' team." Sameer stared coldly at Vijay, who looked away.

"And some of them took the bus back with me. I had a book of tickets in my backpack. Anyway, that's it," he said with relief.

Mrs. Lee sighed and ran her hand over her hair.

"All right, thank you, Sameer and Vijay. You can head back to class now, boys. And this whole thing? Absolutely hush-hush. Got me?"

They nodded and escaped.

SIX
Evasive Action

"Sameer, do you think we'll get in trouble with Coach Boss?" whispered Vijay, grabbing Sameer's arm when they were in the hall. "Seriously. Do you? I mean, the guy's not exactly rational."

"Or even stable," Sameer said. Like Vijay, he was starting to worry.

When they'd been in Mrs. Lee's office, it had been easy to spill everything. Mrs. Lee had encouraged them. They'd almost forgotten that Coach Boss was actually in the school, pretending to teach, unaware that he was being ratted out. Now, outside the safety of the principal's office, Mrs. Lee was receding, and Coach Boss was looming very large.

Sameer and Vijay looked at each other, and each thought the other looked worried.

"Mrs. Lee said she'd keep what we said confidential," said Sameer firmly. "She said that right off the bat."

"Yeah, she did, she did." Vijay nodded with relief. "Also, fact is, *you* did most of the talking, so…"

Sameer gave Vijay a withering look.

"Nice, Vijay, nice. I only took over because you seem to have trouble with speaking. *Screamier*? I mean, that's not even a word."

"You don't have to get all snotty. All I'm saying is that it was *you*—"

"*Vijay*! Mrs. Lee said she'd keep it all quiet. Obviously, we better shut up about it as well. And we better get back to class."

They had just started walking down the hall when they heard the beep that signaled an announcement was coming.

Mrs. Lee's crisp voice came over the school-wide intercom. "Mr. Bosetti, will you come to the office, please? Mr. Bosetti, to the office."

Vijay and Sameer froze.

"Oh, *man*," whimpered Vijay. "Coach Boss is coming to the office *now*! If he sees us he'll know we…Let's get *out* of here."

They sprinted wildly down the hall, faster than they had ever run in gym class. Vijay looked over his shoulder and slowed down a little so Sameer could keep up with him.

"I was in Language Arts. Where were you?" panted Sameer.

"Math," gasped Vijay.

They rounded the corner, slowing to swerve for a trolley of books outside the library. They were just picking up speed when a huge hand pushed open the door of a classroom up ahead.

Sameer and Vijay skidded to a dead stop.

"Coach Boss," hissed Vijay, his fingers digging into Sameer's arm.

The rest of Coach Boss followed his hand through the door, but his head was turned to yell back into the classroom.

"Page seventy-one!" he boomed. "Get to work. Hey! Tyson! That means *you*. Get it *done*! I'll be back in a minute."

"Sameer," Vijay whimpered, frozen, his eyes huge. Sameer had no time to weigh options. He acted on instinct—*move away from the danger.* He grabbed Vijay's shirt and dragged him back around the corner, quickly scanned the hall and pulled him into a storage closet across from the library. He shut the door softly.

"Gak! That practically choked me!" Vijay staggered back and crashed into a metal pail. It made an impossibly loud clanking noise as it swung around and around. Sameer dropped to his hands and knees, groped in the dark for the pail and stilled it.

"Sorry, sorry, I'll just—"

"Shut. Up," breathed Sameer.

"Right," whispered Vijay. "Gotcha."

They waited, out of breath and hearts hammering, as Coach Boss's heavy footsteps passed the closet and continued down the hall.

"I think he's gone," whispered Sameer after about a minute.

"Are you sure? Like, *sure* sure?"

"How can I be sure? I can't see through doors, Vijay. But he must be down at Mrs. Lee's office by now." His voice was confident, but he had a fleeting, terrifying mental image of Coach Boss crouched outside the closet door. *Ridiculous.*

"Maybe we should just stay here the rest of the day," whispered Vijay. Their eyes had adjusted to the gloom, and he looked around the small room. "I bet we could. I bet nobody would care or even notice. I mean, we'd get hungry, and it kind of stinks in here, and possibly there are spiders, but still..."

"We have to go *now*, while he's in the office, before he comes back," said Sameer in an urgent voice. He turned the handle noiselessly, opened the door a crack and peeked out. "All clear."

"Like, completely, absolutely *clear* clear?"

Sameer ground his teeth and pulled Vijay out of the closet.

They ran past Coach Boss's class, which was loudly and happily *not* working on page seventy-one.

"Math class never looked so good," Vijay said as they finally reached his classroom and he leaned his head on the door.

"I know," Sameer said. "Hey, remember to keep it quiet about talking to Mrs. Lee. Don't say anything to anyone, okay?"

"Gotcha. I'm a vault. See you later, Sameer."

Sameer gratefully slipped back into his Language Arts class and sank into his seat. Everyone looked up, hoping for information, but he just shook his head, as if to say, "It was boring. It was nothing." When everyone had gone back to their work, he took off his glasses and wiped his sleeve across his sweaty face.

He pulled out his book of sports commentary, flipped to the index and looked up the word *coach*. There was a long line of headings under the word, which ranged from the positive *inspiration on the bench* and *role model* to the more negative *useless* and *inept*. Sameer ran his finger down the list. It stopped when he reached *toxic, 324*.

He flipped pages, hunched down in his seat and started to read.

SEVEN
Hush-Hush

"Hey, Sameer," Gracie called at lunch, motioning him over. She was sitting with a group of friends. "So you and Vijay told Mrs. Lee all about the McGee game? How Coach Boss got tossed from the game for firing that ball at Nate's head?"

Sameer ground his teeth, thinking how much he would like to throw a ball at Vijay's head.

"Where did you get that idea?" he asked, a polite frozen smile on his face.

"Vijay told us. He said Mrs. Lee called you guys in for some big conference. He said she was really grateful and promised you guys some kind of reward or something."

Sameer snorted. "Oh yeah, Cadillac Escalades all around! Seriously, Gracie? Does that sound like Mrs. Lee?"

"Not really." Gracie laughed, shaking her glossy hair. "So tell us what happened."

"Look. Mrs. Lee called us down to the office. Nate just happened to mention to his mom what happened, seeing as he arrived home looking like Frankenstein even though we cleaned him up as much as we could, and his mom told Mrs. Lee, even though Nate didn't want her to. We were just, you know, witnesses. Corroborating the evidence." Was *corroborate* the right word? Sameer wondered. Nobody called him on it.

"Well, Coach Boss got in trouble, all right. He got called down to the office," said another girl. "Didn't you hear it?"

"Me? Didn't hear a thing," said Sameer innocently.

"I was in Coach Boss's math class when he got called down," said Simone. "He came back looking like he wanted to *murder* somebody."

"Huh," said Sameer, his hands starting to sweat. "You know," he said desperately, looking around the group of girls, "I'm thinking it'd be great if nobody here tells anybody else about this. Mrs. Lee said she'd keep it confidential, and we were supposed to as well. But Vijay…" Sameer bit back a wave of rage and forced a chuckle. "Well, you know Vijay. Quite a talker. Always has to be a big shot. Always wants to be the big hero."

"Okay, Sameer," said Gracie, looking serious. "We'll keep it secret, right?" Her friends nodded.

"Thanks," said Sameer. "It's not like I don't trust you. It's just, well, you know how rumors get exaggerated around this place. Pretty soon it'll be the cops landing a helicopter on the roof and swarming down the sides of the school to take down Coach Boss!"

The girls laughed.

Sameer walked away feeling happier. He thought he'd handled that pretty well. And Gracie and her friends had said they wouldn't tell anyone else. He could trust them. Maybe this thing could be contained so it didn't reach Coach Boss. He'd just gotten to his locker and reached for his lock when his friend Desmond ran in from outside. He saw Sameer and ran straight over.

·"Sameer, I heard Coach Boss half killed a few guys on the basketball team in the middle of the McGee game and is going to prison!"

Sameer closed his eyes and banged his head gently on his locker.

"Hey, Desmond, do you know where Vijay is?" he asked through gritted teeth.

EIGHT
Just Managing

"Sameer. Sa*meer*!" Gracie hissed the next morning, motioning him over to her locker.

Oh no, what now? he thought. He trotted over, alarmed at the urgency in her tone. "Simone says they have a *substitute teacher* in math." She looked at him expectantly.

Sameer stared back in confusion. Why were they talking about Simone's substitute teacher?

"Well, you can sometimes goof off with a sub," he said.

Gracie crossed her arms and rolled her eyes. "Think, Sameer, *think*! A sub. For Coach *Boss*! He's gone!"

"*What*? What do you mean, *gone*? You mean, like, taking a day off?"

"Nope. *Gone*," Gracie said. "The sub said she was there *indefinitely*. So Boss has been fired or is on stress leave or is taking anger-management courses or something. Who knows? But he's gone! Must have been the McGee game. And you and Vijay ratting him out to Mrs. Lee."

"We didn't *rat him out*, as you so elegantly put it," Sameer protested, using air quotes around the offending phrase. He pushed up his glasses and shifted his backpack. "We told the truth. You'd have done the same thing if you'd been there. Seriously, Gracie, the man has problems. You've seen him. You know how he's been treating the guys on the team."

"I know, I know. It's been super ugly for a while. Glad I was in the other gym, watching the girls' team hammer McGee."

"Wow, they beat McGee?" Sameer asked, momentarily sidetracked.

"By eighteen."

"Holy *cow*. Blowout."

"Yeah, everybody played great. Especially Janessa and Kayley. I think they'll be city champs this year, I really do."

"Beat McGee," Sameer said, marveling. "The guys got slaughtered by fifty-seven points. Gracie, have you ever wondered why the girls' team, uh—"

"Rocks? While the guys' team sucks?" interrupted Gracie.

"Wouldn't have put it *quite* like that, but yeah."

Gracie thought about it. "It's not height or speed or anything. Or even talent. Bad coaching has done something to their confidence. It's..." She pointed to her head.

"Mental! Psychological! That's what I think too," said Sameer.

"Oh well, not our problem," said Gracie. "Gotta go."

Sameer looked after her, thinking. Disjointed thoughts snaked through his mind.

She's right, it's not my problem.

On the other hand, it's going to be somebody's problem.

It's mental. Psychological.

Those guys are my friends.

Somebody's going to have to take over, and they'll need a heads-up about the team.

Find your place, Sameer—dig in, and dig deep.

Sameer made a decision. He headed to his locker, dumped his backpack and pulled out a huge red binder. It had *Gladiators Basketball* written in black felt pen on the front. He smoothed a hand over it, tucked it under his arm and headed for the office.

"Mrs. Lee? Yep, she's in. Gets here early." The secretary smiled, which seemed like a good sign. "Head on back."

Mrs. Lee was frowning at her computer but looked up as Sameer appeared in the doorway.

"Sameer. Come in. Sit."

"That's okay, Mrs. Lee. I won't be long. I just wanted to give you this." He handed her the binder.

"Oof. It's huge," she said, setting it down with a *thunk* on the desk. "What is it?"

"Information. About the Gladiators basketball team. It's organized according to player stats, team stats, performance against league teams, trends, projections—stuff like that."

Mrs. Lee's eyebrows rose. "Wow. You are quite a fan, Sameer."

Sameer shrugged. "Well, they're my friends, and the stats are kind of a hobby, I guess. I heard about Coach Bosetti taking…uh…some time off, and I thought the binder might help whoever takes over the coaching of the team. You know, get them up to speed. Give them some info."

Mrs. Lee sat back in her chair and smiled. "That was very thoughtful of you, Sameer."

There was an awkward silence. Sameer pushed up his glasses.

"Well, I better go…"

"Hold on, Sameer. Just a second. I'm a basketball fan too. You probably didn't know that," Mrs. Lee said.

"No. No, I didn't. I mean, I've seen you at the games, obviously."

"Big Lakers fan."

Sameer winced sympathetically. "Tough season this year."

"Yeah, it sucks. Anyway, I have too many responsibilities—the school renovations, the new academic programs, fundraising for the upgrades to the gym, the *roof*..." Mrs. Lee sighed and rubbed her forehead. "Otherwise I'd coach the team myself. And all of the staff are already at a full admin load as well."

Sameer got a wobbly feeling. It was the middle of the basketball season, but Mrs. Lee was sounding pretty negative here.

"You're not saying the team's just going to fold!" Sameer said. "Cancel the rest of the season? That just wouldn't be fair to the players, to a great bunch of guys who have practiced so hard and who love basketball."

"Hey, hey." Mrs. Lee held up her hands. "Not so fast, Sameer. I'm *hoping* we can find a coach," she said. "I have one staff member left to approach. But everyone's super busy. It's a long shot. It would help if I could tell them they would have a very competent team manager." She looked directly at Sameer.

Sameer felt dazed. *Manager.*

"Me?" he said, pointing a finger at his chest, his heart thumping.

"You."

Sameer was speechless. It was more than he'd ever hoped for. His mind whirled. Gracie, the manager of the girls' team, could commentate the boys' games, and he could do the girls' games, and Vijay could score…

"Absolutely, Mrs. Lee. I would be honored. Sign me up. Anytime," Sameer said quickly, before she changed her mind.

"Great!" Mrs. Lee stood up. "Give me a day to approach the staff member. I'll get back to you. Otherwise we'll have to start asking parents," she said. "And nobody wants that."

They both contemplated this possibility unenthusiastically. Only two or three parents ever showed up at the games, and none of them appeared to be even close to coach material.

"Yeah, the guys probably wouldn't want that," said Sameer, a vision of blotchy Mrs. Schneider yelling from the bench flitting through his mind.

"I know. I'll do what I can."

"Great. Thanks, Mrs. Lee. Oh," Sameer said, "one last thing. Who's the teacher you have in mind to be the new coach?"

"Nope. Out." Mrs. Lee was shaking her head and making shooing motions with her hands. "Thanks for the binder, Sameer. I'll let you know."

NINE
Substitution

"...**A**nd finally, Gladiators boys' basketball team, there will be basketball practice as usual today after school. Enjoy your day." A metallic click ended the morning announcements.

Sameer sat up and looked over his shoulder at Vijay, one desk back, who was already pawing through his lunch.

"Must mean we just got ourselves a coach, Mr. Manager," Vijay said through a bite of chicken wrap. Sameer had spent all Sunday evening on his computer, coming up with a practice schedule that balanced shooting, defense drills, offensive and inbounding plays, and scrimmaging. He had printed out the pages and secured them neatly on a clipboard. The new coach was not going to think his team manager was a slacker.

Sameer and Vijay were eating with a few guys from the team during lunch break. Rochon and Anil, the team's only ninth-graders, were not exactly doing cartwheels over the prospect of a new coach.

"It'll probably be some reject," said Anil. "Seriously, any decent coach wouldn't be caught dead picking up a team three-quarters of the way through the season."

"Half," said Sameer. "Closer to half."

"Whatever. I've got a bad feeling about this," said Rochon. "Anyway, what's the point? Whole team sucks anyway. Half the guys shouldn't be anywhere near a basketball team."

"Ah, guys, don't be so negative. Coach Boss was a terrible coach. *Toxic*. He's undermined everyone's confidence. There's lots of talent on this team. We just have to focus and—"

"Sameer," said Anil intently. "We *suck*. Most of the team is garbage. Accept it."

Most of the other guys from the team sat in silence.

Anil and Rochon got up to go. "Later, guys."

"Wait!" Vijay said.

Thank you, Vijay, thought Sameer. Give them some old gladiator spirit.

"You're not going to eat that?" Vijay asked, pointing to the half-eaten granola bar Anil was aiming at the garbage can. Sameer's heart sank.

"Make a hoop," Anil instructed. It was an old game they played. Lethal objects aside, pretty much anything could be thrown through the body hoop. Vijay dutifully linked his arms in a big circle and turned his face away.

Anil aimed and shot the granola bar straight in.

"Two points!" said Sameer. "Drained it. From, what? Fifteen feet? Not bad, Anil. Nothing like basketball, hey? Nothing like it. See you at practice," he called after them.

"Forget them, Sameer," Kyle said, scraping up the last of his yogurt with a plastic spoon. "Coach Boss wasn't the only toxic one on the team."

Nikho and Nate nodded.

Sameer looked over at Kyle. "Yeah, but things will be better now. A decent coach, some structured practices, a fresh start, right?"

Kyle shrugged. "Sure, Sameer. Whatever."

"So where's the new coach?" Vijay asked Sameer after school, looking around the empty gym. He had badgered Sameer into making him assistant manager, which involved filling water bottles, promising to take detailed game stats and bragging about being assistant manager.

Sameer looked up from his clipboard. He had been studying his practice plan during health class and was making some final adjustments. He checked the clock over the scoreboard.

"Early yet," he said. "He'll be here. The guys won't be here for another ten minutes."

"Hope he's a good guy," said Vijay. "Or maybe it's not a *guy*. Maybe it's a *girl*."

"Yeah, maybe it is. Whatever. Someone like Ms. Morrison would be great." The coach of the Gladiators girls' team had played university basketball and knew the game inside out.

"What if it's somebody like Mrs. Woznicki?" Vijay said idly.

In spite of his resolution to stay calm and professional, Sameer panicked.

"Why would you say that? It's not going to be Mrs. Wosnicki! I'm sure she has zero interest in coaching basketball. Plus, she's, well…"

"Ancient?" Vijay suggested. "Well, who then? Bantu does volleyball, Schultz is hockey, Forman's soccer." Vijay listed off the teachers on his fingers.

Sameer shrugged dismissively. But he's right, he thought hopelessly. There's nobody. He had run through all the staff the night before, and the ones even remotely athletic already coached other sports.

"Mrs. Lee knows what she's doing. And she knows basketball."

Vijay raised his eyebrows. "Really."

"Lakers fan," said Sameer.

The lifelong Lakers haters looked at each other and shrugged.

When they heard voices in the hallway, Sameer and Vijay moved to the gym door and looked through the window. Mrs. Lee was walking down the hallway, talking to two men.

"Ho*ly*. That guy must be, what, six nine? Six ten?" Vijay breathed, grabbing Sameer's arm. "Wow. That is tall. Like, *tall* tall. Never seen anybody that size in real life! I have a good feeling about this, Sameer!"

"Ah, Sameer. Vijay. Just the men we were looking for," Mrs. Lee said. "I'd like to introduce you to the Gladiators' new coach, Mr. Williams."

Sameer held out his hand to the huge man with the clipboard. "Great to meet you, sir."

"Uh…" The man looked down at Sameer, at Sameer's hand, confusion clouding his face. He looked over at Mrs. Lee.

"Oh, sorry, Sameer. Not him. That's Dan. He's doing the school's renovations. *This*—" she turned and gestured to the small, slight young man nobody had noticed "—*this* is Mr. Williams."

Mr. Williams tucked his curly, shoulder -length brown hair behind his ears, stepped forward and reached for Sameer's hand. He had a surprisingly firm grip.

"I am assured that he's *not* a screamer," said Mrs. Lee with a laugh as Mr. Williams shook Vijay's hand.

"Absolutely not," said Mr. Williams seriously. "I've hated loud noises since I was a child."

There was an awkward pause. Sameer and Vijay glanced at each other, then looked away.

"Mr. Williams is the new ninth grade Language Arts teacher. He really wants to start up a school drama program soon," Mrs. Lee said. "He's got big plans! I'm sure he'll try to recruit you boys to the new Dramatic Society," she warned.

"Ah," said Sameer, wondering if his frozen smile looked in any way normal.

"And it's so good of him to take on coaching the basketball team as well. It looks like they're waiting for you," Mrs. Lee said to Mr. Williams. "Have fun, Aubry. They're a good group. Dan, let's have a look at that retaining wall…"

As they began walking into the gym, Mr. Williams turned to Sameer. "I have to thank you, Sameer, for your magnificent opus!"

"Ah," mumbled Sameer, confused. *Opus*?

"So detailed and thorough! You have a real gift for description."

Oh, he means the stats binder, thought Sameer. "Glad to help out," he said.

"I really feel I have a good grasp of the cast of characters already," Mr. Williams enthused, "and I haven't even met them yet."

"Good. That's good," said Sameer.

"So, Mr. Williams," said Vijay, "do you play any sports?"

"Sadly, no longer," Mr. Williams confessed, running a hand through his hair.

Sameer said quickly and with relief, "But you did? You did play some sports before?"

"Oh yes."

"Basketball?"

"Fencing, actually. While technically horse racing is the sport of kings, I've always felt it should be fencing!" He mimed a flourish with an imaginary sword. Sensing this was not the answer they were looking for, he added, "Also, I've played darts a little."

"Ah," said Sameer. "Pointy sports. Anything with a ball?"

Mr. Williams considered this with narrowed eyes, looking off into the distance. "I seem to remember…wait! Of course! Croquet!" he said triumphantly. "But, full disclosure, that was *years and years* ago. In England."

"Ah."

While Mr. Williams explained what croquet was to a mystified Vijay, Sameer quickly walked ahead to the group of guys clustered at the end of the gym.

"Where'd the big guy with the clipboard go, Sameer?" said Nikho, craning to look over Sameer's shoulder.

"To do some school renovations. He's not the coach." Sameer cleared his throat and spoke a little louder. "Guys! Listen up. *That* is our new coach." He pointed back at Mr. Williams, who was enthusiastically swinging an imaginary croquet mallet as Vijay looked on.

"What, the pale little guy with the long hair and the purple shirt?" said Anil. The rest of the team turned to look. "He looks ten years old. *I* have more facial hair."

"Coach Williams is stepping up so the team won't have to fold," said Sameer, his eyes on the floor. "We should be thanking him. *Thanking* him."

Silence.

"Seriously? Did I miss something?" said Rochon. "We're talking about the scrawny little guy talking to Vijay? Oh, this is *perfect*." He started to laugh. A few others joined in.

Sameer rounded on them. "Yeah, and Coach Boss, the big sports guy, was such a prize, hey, Anil? Hey, Rochon?"

"Id he dice, Sabeer?" asked Nate. His nose was still swollen, and he peered down at Sameer with two black eyes.

Sameer turned to him with relief. "Yes. Yes, he seems nice, Nate. Teaches drama, so maybe he'll bring a little creativity"—he raised his voice over some of the team mutterings—"yes, *creativity* to this team! And Mrs. Lee says he's definitely not a screamer."

"Dat's someding," said Nate, nodding.

"Does he know anything about basketball?" asked Kyle, who had been studying the new coach out of the corner of his eye.

"He's not a screamer," repeated Sameer firmly, turning away.

TEN
Team Motto

Mr. Williams came over to the group, smiling.

"So, Mr. Williams," Sameer said. "*Coach* Williams. Everybody's here. Should we maybe start a warm-up or something?"

"Thank you, Sameer, but I think a small introduction is in order," Mr. Williams said, facing the team. He paused for a moment, looked down and put a finger to his lips.

"*To be, or not to be*," he said in a loud, theatrical voice, making several guys jump. "*That* was the question Mrs. Lee put to me. Whether this team would continue to play or quietly wither away." He made a fluttery gesture with his fingers. "I chose *to be*!"

There was a silence.

Oh, *man*, this is awful, thought Sameer, squirming.

Vijay clapped twice uncertainly, looked around at the stunned faces of the guys on the team, then crossed his arms.

"Well, good," said Sameer. "That's good. Great."

"Is that poetry?" asked Kenneth in his deep voice.

"Id's Hablet, iddn't id?" Nate asked, surprising everyone.

"Indeed, the quotation is from *Hamlet*," Mr. Williams said, his face lighting up. "Shakespeare is my specialty! Are you a fan?" he asked Nate.

Nate looked a little embarrassed and shook his head.

"I'll let you all in on an exciting secret," Mr. Williams said conspiratorially. "The newly formed Gladys Spinoza Dramatic Society will be performing a version of *Henry V*, one of Shakespeare's classics!"

"And what's the exciting secret?" said Vijay.

Mr. Williams's face fell. "Well, that's it. That we're doing *Henry V*. I just decided on the play last night and began preparatory work. It's a thrilling play of courage and heroism and intrigue!"

Vijay slid a hand around the back of his thin neck. "My brother said we don't have to do Shakespeare until tenth grade."

"*That* is a pity, Vijay, because when you study Shakespeare, you learn about the great themes of life, you learn about the richness of the English language, you learn about the world. And knowledge, after all, is *the wing wherewith we fly to heaven*!"

Anil muttered, "Oh, man" and stared down at his shoes, shaking his head. Rochon whispered something to him, and they both bit back smiles.

"Cool," said Sameer. "Very interesting. And good luck with that performance, Coach. Now, I'm thinking that we should probably get practising." He tapped his watch. "Almost four o'clock! We only have the gym until five."

"Of course, of course," said Mr. Williams, smiling. "I was forgetting why we're here. By all means, we should take to the pitch." He made an awkward gesture, swinging his arm out. On a wave of relief, the guys fanned out, dribbling basketballs and shooting. Mr. Williams called over the noise, "I'm delighted to be standing in as coach, and I hope you'll bear with me while I get to know you all and master the rules."

"Warm up for five minutes, and then we'll do a shooting drill," called Sameer.

Mr. Williams rubbed his hands together and looked over at Sameer with a smile, his pale face slightly flushed. "I thought that went very well, didn't you?" he said.

Mr. Williams let Sameer run the practice. He seemed happy to watch, sitting on the bench with his elbows on his knees. He pulled Sameer's binder out of his backpack and every once in a while he consulted it, nodding his head, squinting off into the distance or smiling to himself.

The last twenty minutes of practice was a scrimmage, with Vijay pretending to ref, a whistle clenched in his big teeth.

When five o'clock rolled around, Mr. Williams got up and called out, "All right, boys, huddle up! That was a good little game thingy you were playing!"

"Scrimmage," said Sameer quickly. "It's called a scrimmage."

"Thank you, Sameer. Everyone have a seat." Mr. Williams indicated the bench.

Sameer's heart sank as he squeezed in between the twins, Hassan and Mohammed. *Another squirm-inducing speech? More Shakespeare?* He looked down the bench. Anil and Rochon, their faces hard and set, had their arms crossed.

"I ask for three minutes to see whether I've got things right," Mr. Williams said. He walked quickly to the end of the bench and began a rapid-fire commentary, gesturing with both arms at each player as he went down the line.

"Rochon and Anil, elder statesmen of the team, ninth-graders, talented marksmen, a little lazy on defending their own basket and prone to a touch of arrogance, but excellent leadership capabilities." Before either player could even register the description, he had moved on.

"Kyle, a quiet tower of strength, a calming presence and a solid player needing only the confidence to be a leader in his own way." Mr. Williams moved down the bench.

"Nate, Big Nate, whose towering frame is matched only by the magnitude of his heart. Be not afraid of your size, good Nate—*use* your Olympian stature!

"Nikho, deft and quick. Your physical skill is apparent. Work on the mental element of concentration to finish the job. Plus, incidentally, I admire your most excellent faux-hawk.

"Tom, a player who needs to rise from the bench and take his place! For too long you have been unappreciated and your abilities minimized." Tom sat up a little straighter.

"Kenneth, questioning Kenneth, your athleticism almost brought tears to my eyes. Work with your teammates, and you will indeed be formidable.

"Hassan and Mohammed." Mr. Williams gestured to the twins. "You do share an astonishing likeness, and it's virtually impossible to tell you apart at a glance. No matter. As the only two representatives of seventh grade, you will both learn and grow and will begin to assert your individuality.

"Sameer, excellent Sameer! You have the qualities of organization, strategy and the natural leadership of a general in the field! I hereby promote you to assistant coach." Sameer blinked and stared.

"And, finally, Vijay, fearless mascot, scorer and assistant to the manager…"

"Assistant manager," said Vijay. "But willing to be promoted!"

"Manager it is! Your easygoing good nature will prove invaluable to this team."

There was a moment of silence.

"Gladiators," cried Mr. Williams, "disperse!"

"Okay, that's it for today, guys," said Sameer as the team hesitated.

Everyone headed for the gym doors.

"I'll just get my backpack, and we'll head out," said Vijay to Sameer.

Sameer nodded. "I'll wait here."

He sat on the bench, clutching his clipboard and trying not to think about the rest of the season. Mr. Williams had nailed the player descriptions, but Sameer knew some of the guys wouldn't appreciate that. They would just fixate on the fact that he was odd. He *was* odd. But was he odd enough that the whole rest of the season was going to be a nightmare?

Exhausted and confused, he stared off into space in the silent gym. His eyes fell on the Gladiators logo painted on the gym wall. It was a helmeted head in black silhouette against a red circle background crossed by two swords. Underneath the head was a stenciled motto:

Our strength does not lie in not failing, but in getting up every single time we fail.

I wonder if Coach Boss actually wrote that, Sameer thought. Or did he just read it somewhere? Anyway, who writes an inspirational quote that mentions failing not once, but twice?

Mr. Williams trotted back into the gym.

"Forgot this." He smiled, grabbing Sameer's red binder from under the bench. "Everything all right, Sameer?" He followed Sameer's gaze and read the quote Sameer was staring at. Mr. Williams tilted his head. "That's somehow not a terribly inspirational phrase, is it?"

"I was just thinking that."

"It hints at the value of perseverance but seems to dwell darkly and repetitively on failure."

"Yeah," said Sameer, "I noticed that."

"Shakespeare would have said it better," said Mr. Williams.

Sameer looked up, interested in spite of himself. *Shakespeare wrote about sports?*

"What would he have said about the Gladiators?"

Mr. Williams tilted his head, looking up at the ceiling and thinking. "Oh, I know! This is a good one: *We know what we are, but know not what we may be.*"

Sameer considered this. "You're right, that *is* better. Way better."

Mr. Williams smiled and nodded. "See you later, Sameer. And thanks for running the...you know...the rehearsal!"

"Practice."

"*Practice*," Mr. Williams repeated eagerly. "Practice. Of course." He smiled and gave an awkward little salute.

When Mr. Williams had gone, Sameer wrote out the quotation on the top of his practice notes.

We know what we are, but know not what we may be.

That's a great team motto, Sameer thought. He hauled his big book of sports commentary out of his backpack, looked up *mottos* in the index and flipped to page 232, wondering whether Shakespeare had made the list.

ELEVEN
Maintaining Composure

"**H**e's an idiot," Rochon said a few days later when they were shooting baskets at lunch.

"Yeah, a guy who can quote endless Shakespeare off the top of his head is a real idiot," Sameer said sarcastically.

"Okay, maybe not an idiot. A freak?"

"Bit harsh," said Sameer. "He's a little different maybe."

"He doesn't have a clue about basketball," said Anil, spinning the ball on one finger. Sameer had nothing to say to that. It was true. "Not the smallest clue. All that deep breathing we do in practice? The yoga stretches? It's ridiculous."

"I know for a fact that lots of NBA players do yoga," said Sameer, wagging a finger, "for the flexibility."

"I touched my toes for the first time last practice," said Hassan (or Mohammed). He looked around, nodding with pride. "So maybe the yoga works."

"Good," said Sameer. "That's great...uh... Hassan."

"Mohammed."

Rochon ignored both of them. "Seriously. What good is a stupid downward-dog pose going to be against J.P. Thorpe tomorrow? They're going to murder us."

There was an uneasy silence.

"Anybody else find Williams embarrassing?" asked Anil. "I came out of Science, and he says, in front of everyone, *'The curtain rises on our athletic ballet at 4:00 PM.'* Anil said it in an exaggerated, dramatic way. A few of the guys laughed. "Like, meaning basketball practice." Anil looked around, his hands held out. "I mean, what do you even *say* to that? 'Uh, *yeah*, later, *Coach*.' All that Shakespeare garbage. Why can't he just talk normal?"

"Okay, he is a little…dramatic. That's true," said Sameer.

"*Really* dramatic," said Vijay. "Like *DRA-matic*!" He flung out his arms.

"Thanks, Vijay," said Sameer wearily. "He is a drama teacher, after all. But he's a smart guy. Anyway, we don't have a choice, right? He's who we got. There's nobody else."

"I never, *ever* thought I would miss Coach Boss," said Rochon. "But hey, can we get him back? I mean, he was a total jerk, but with him there was a tiny chance we might actually win. Or at least not be humiliated."

"Really?" said Sameer. "I seem to remember lots of humiliation with Coach Boss. A lot of it. Humiliation, bullying, intimidation." He listed them on his fingers.

"Sameer's right," said Mohammed (or Hassan).

"But he wasn't a total freak," Anil said slowly, emphasizing each word.

"Dot so fast," said Nate. "Coach Will mide be odd, but he's *dice*."

"Yeah," said Kyle. "I got no problems with him. Well, maybe I could do without the singing. But other than that…"

"See, that's the kind of thing I mean," wailed Anil. "There's a game tomorrow, and the guy's going to humiliate us. It's bad enough that we *suck*. We don't need to be *humiliated* as well. And I'm not even mentioning his hair or his clothes."

"Hey, hold it right there," said Vijay aggressively, pointing a finger at Anil. "I think Coach Will rocks a very cool look. Sort of a goth-poet vibe."

"There you go," said Anil, like Vijay had made his point for him.

"Okay, okay, I got it, I got it," said Sameer. "Can't do anything about the way he looks, but I'll try to talk to him about the yoga and the singing. And the quoting."

But Sameer was worried. *How do you tell a person to try not to be himself?*

TWELVE
Game Plan

Gracie sat with Sameer on the bus after the game against J.P. Thorpe. It happened in an accidental way, with a whole group of them piling onto the bus and fanning out for seats. Gracie just crashed in beside him, but Sameer wasn't complaining.

Gracie and her friends had asked to come along on the team bus to watch the game, and Coach Will had said, "The more the merrier!" which was a refreshing change from Coach Boss's belligerent "Team-only" policy.

"I'm impressed you can actually drive this bus, Coach," Vijay said. "I mean, legally. Like, you *can* drive it legally, right? 'Cause you don't really strike me as a big machine guy." He was asking what all of them were thinking.

"Oh yes, rest assured, Vijay," Coach Will said, "I'm fully licensed. Completely legal. I taught band at my last school and drove the group to performances, tubas and all." He leaned on the steering wheel, reminiscing. "Now that group had some wonderful sing-alongs." He glanced in the rearview mirror, saw Sameer's face and said, "Not that I'm suggesting *this* group should have sing-alongs."

Sameer relaxed into his seat. Coach Will was learning. "Well, another loss, hey, Sameer," Gracie said, idly kicking at the seatback in front of her.

"Yep." Sameer nodded. "Depressing."

"Not a bad loss though," she said.

"What do you mean?"

She turned to face him. Her dancing brown eyes were serious for a moment. "Well, every guy got in the game, so it was way more of a team effort than it's ever been before."

"Yeah, I really like that about Coach Will. Gives everyone a chance." He didn't mention that Rochon and Anil had complained bitterly to him after the game about that very policy. They were not happy to sit on the bench and take turns.

"What else did you notice about the game, Gracie? You know basketball. I really want to hear what you think. Some of the guys aren't happy, and I'm helping coach the team. Vijay's helping too. Team manager." Sameer thought he should put in a word for his friend. Sameer had been so busy trying to keep everyone happy, he hadn't had much of a chance to concentrate on the game, so he really hoped Vijay had taken diligent stats as instructed. Somehow he doubted it. He looked over his shoulder and found Vijay sitting at the back of the bus. He was sandwiched between Hassan and Mohammed, glaring at Sameer.

"Passing was good," said Gracie, "but Rochon and Anil are total ball hogs. They only pass to each other and don't give anyone else a chance to shoot. I mean, Anil stripped the ball right off Nate a couple of times! His own *player*."

"Yeah, I saw that. Our defense also sucked," said Sameer.

"Yes, *defense*," Gracie said. "Guys always want the big dunk, the three-pointer or the steal. All the flashy glamor stuff, but they're out there standing still on defense, getting burned. They gotta *move*."

Sameer smiled. "You're absolutely right, Gracie. I'll make a note to work on that in practice. Are you an NBA fan? I mean, you sure know a lot about basketball. You got a favorite team?"

"Celtics," Gracie said. Sameer was glad she was rummaging in her backpack so he had time to get his face under control.

His nani would have liked Gracie. Her beloved Celtics had another outspoken fan.

"You want a piece of gum?" Gracie asked.

"Thanks."

They sat silently chewing, one of them happier than he'd been in a long time.

THIRTEEN
Fancy Footwork

"Vijay, what on earth is *this*?" Sameer asked, pointing to a bunch of squiggles on the stats chart he had created to make Vijay's stats collecting foolproof.

"No idea," said Vijay, barely glancing over. They were sitting on the bench in the gym, waiting for practice. Vijay had his arms crossed and his face turned away from Sameer.

Sameer nudged Vijay with his elbow. "And this one. What's *this* one? Seriously, could you look at it?" Sameer pointed with his pen at another cryptic squiggle.

Vijay glanced at the squiggle. "I don't know. A three? An eight? Maybe it's a star. I don't know."

"A star? The column is for number of rebounds. What would a star even mean?"

Vijay shrugged. "Look, Sameer, I don't know if you've noticed, but the game goes pretty fast, okay? I've only got, like, a couple of eyes and hands."

"That's why I tried to make it easier—"

"You know what? I'm not talking to you. I'm *mad* at you, if you haven't noticed, Mr. Robotic Stats… Guy." Vijay floundered a little on this description. Then he blurted out, "You couldn't have changed places with me on the bus?"

Sameer put his pen down. "So *that's* what all this is about. Gracie sitting with me on the bus?"

"Would it have killed you to help out a friend, Sameer? Your *best* friend since *kindergarten*? I'd have helped you out in a heartbeat, in a second, in a nanosecond. In a"—he paused, searching for the right word—"*hyper*second!" Sameer opened his mouth, then thought he'd better let that one go. "Anyway," finished Vijay, "I'd have helped you out."

"What was I supposed to do, Vijay? Stand up and flag you down? Whistle you over? Crawl over everyone to change seats with you? You were all the way at the back of the bus. She just sat beside me at the last second before the bus pulled away." And I enjoyed every minute of it, he thought, feeling a little guilty.

"Did she at least mention me?" Vijay asked.

"Your name came up, yes," said Sameer, looking down at his shoes.

Vijay perked up. "Excellent." He looked at Sameer. "Well? Go on. I'm listening."

"Um, well, I mentioned what a good manager you are. I hadn't seen your stats yet."

"Well, that's something. *Manager* sounds impressive." Vijay sighed. "So unfair. I get stuck between two sweaty, stinking players, and you get half an hour of laughing and talking with Gracie. I *saw* you. Laughing. Talking. Man, you know I like her. Like, *like* like her."

"You've *like* liked pretty much every girl in eighth grade this year. A few in seventh and ninth as well."

"This is different," Vijay said. "Soooo different. I've liked Gracie for, what?" He squinted his eyes reflectively. "Ten days now. Ten whole days, Sameer. The best ten days of my life."

Sameer was relieved to hear the gym door bang open.

"*...and I polished up that handle so carefully that now I am the ruler of the Queen's navy!*" They swiveled around. Mr. Williams had come into the gym, singing and carrying a bunch of badminton rackets.

"Hello, boys." He dumped the rackets on the floor in front of Sameer. "Had a dickens of a time finding these. Seventh-graders had them."

"Uh, you coaching badminton now too, Coach Will?" Vijay asked.

"Oh no." Mr. Williams laughed, pushing back his hair. "I'm *terrible* at racket sports. I can never coordinate the racket to actually hit the ball or that little feathered thingy."

"Birdie," said Sameer, looking down at the pile of rackets.

"Right. The birdsie. No, these are for basketball practice. I know, I know," he said, holding up a hand when he saw their faces. "You're thinking, 'What on earth is this fellow up to now?'"

"Heh-heh, pretty much," Sameer said, glancing at Vijay.

"But there's *method in my madness*, I assure you. Don't say a word to the others." Mr. Williams rubbed his hands, smiled down at Vijay and Sameer, and bustled off to pull the wheeled bin of basketballs out of equipment storage.

Oh, we won't say anything, thought Sameer as Rochon and Anil came into the gym. We certainly won't.

Sameer gathered up the rackets and shoved them behind the bench.

"Yeah yeah, good idea," Vijay whispered. "Maybe he'll forget about them. You want me to toss my hoodie over them?"

"Absolutely."

When the team arrived for practice, Mr. Williams called them in.

"Now, my fine young Gladiators, having studied your performance at yesterday's game, I find some very promising things."

"Promising?" said Anil. "Are you kidding? We lost. Bad. Again."

"Yes, that's true." Mr. Williams waved a hand dismissively. "But there were definitely positive developments. For example…"

This is a nice change, thought Sameer as Mr. Williams paced back and forth, enumerating the things the team had done well. Several of the guys were looking stunned. *I'll bet Coach Boss never started the practice after a loss with any kind of positive feedback. I'm guessing every post-game practice was hard running. Pure torture.*

"Nice not to run suicides, hey?" he whispered to Rochon, who shrugged.

"And having said all that," concluded Mr. Williams, with an awkward clap, "I am reminded that *words are not deeds*. We still have work to do! There was a certain amount of, well, sluggishness on defense," he said almost apologetically. "A flat-footedness, where the opposing team simply swept around, unhindered." He made a sweeping motion with his arm.

He's right, thought Sameer, surprised. Gracie said the same thing. She said it with way less goofy words, but still...

"So I thought we might try a creative exercise to get our brains and our feet working together." Mr. Williams became brisk. "Sameer, where are those rackets?"

"Ah, they must've just got pushed back here behind the bench. And somehow this hoodie fell on top of them." Sameer stepped over the bench and gathered up the badminton rackets. He hesitated.

"Well, what are we waiting for?" Mr. Williams cried, gesturing toward Sameer. "Grab one, everyone. Seize the rackets!"

"We're playing badminton?" asked Kenneth.

"No, Kenneth. We are"—Mr. Williams grabbed a racket, bent his knees and held it out like a sword—"*fencing*! For lack of any swords, these rackets will have to do." He quick-stepped toward Kenneth, who held up his racket protectively. Kenneth was way taller, but Mr. Williams was quick. "Good, good! Footwork! That's the stuff of fencing! Moving…of…the…feet." Mr. Williams dodged and darted at Kenneth, brandishing his racket. "Anticipation! Reflex!" Kenneth staggered back, flailing his racket to deflect the onslaught.

"It is…not…about—Got you there!—the sword…or the racket in this instance," panted Mr. Williams. "It is—yes, Kenneth, touché!—all…in…the *feet*!" He stopped and turned to the rest of the team. "Go on, you lot! Have a go!"

Sameer glanced quickly at the rest of the team. Anil and Rochon dangled their rackets, looking angry. Hassan and Mohammed, their faces serious, held theirs up to each other, looking like a mirror image. Kenneth and Kyle faced off, Vijay jumped in enthusiastically to thrash at Tom, and Nikho flailed away nimbly at Nate, who lurched backward awkwardly, fending off his far shorter friend.

"I'b glad these aren't real swords."

"C'mon, that would be *way* more fun! Could you even *imagine* how much fun…that…would…be?" Nikho punctuated his words with thrusts and slashes.

"Excellent! Move those feet! Keep up with your opponent!" Mr. Williams coached from the sidelines. "Small, controlled movements!"

Sameer noticed uneasily that a few of the players from the girls' team were watching from the door, talking and laughing. We should have shut that door, thought Sameer. And locked it.

Mr. Williams finally came over to Rochon and Anil, who were standing still, watching the others with disgust. "Rochon, Anil? Not going to try? It's a pity. As Shakespeare said, *Our doubts are traitors, and make us lose the good we oft might win, by fearing to attempt."*

"Okay, that's it." Anil threw down his racket, causing a clatter that startled the others into stillness. "This is so STUPID!" he yelled.

Mr. Williams made an involuntary gesture to cover his ears but stopped himself.

"Anil's right," said Rochon, throwing his racket down too. "All this," he gestured in disgust, "the fencing, the quoting—all of it's stupid. It has nothing, *nothing* to do with basketball."

"C'bon, guys," said Nate uncertainly. "It's dot that bad—"

"Yeah, Nate, it is," Anil said. "You guys are pathetic. You can't even see how bad it is."

"Okay, okay," said Sameer, rushing in to intervene. "You don't want to do this drill. You want to sit this one out. You made your point."

"No, I don't think I have, Sameer," said Anil. "This isn't a *drill*. This is more useless garbage wasting the time of this loser team, and this guy," he gestured at Mr. Williams, "is already getting us laughed at. Face it, guys. This team is one big humiliation." He looked over at the girls by the door and called, "Having a good laugh, ladies? Funny, right?" They scattered.

"Anil—" Mr. Williams said.

"Forget it." Anil turned away. "Just forget it. I'm done with this team. I quit."

"Me too," said Rochon. "Good luck, guys. You'll need it."

Anil and Rochon grabbed their bags and slammed out the gym door.

FOURTEEN
Back on Track?

The sound of the gym door slamming faded into a dead silence.

This is bad, this is so bad, thought Sameer, closing his eyes.

Some of the boys eyed each other uncertainly. Some stared at the floor.

Sameer cleared his throat and said matter-of-factly, "I'll talk to them. It's nothing. They're blowing off a little steam, that's all. Niners, right?" He looked around, wondering if he was being convincing. "Maybe I should go after them. Should I go after them?"

"Nah. You're wasting your time, Sameer," said Kyle.

"Maybe if I just explain—"

"Sameer, you know those two have been threatening to quit since…for a while."

Since Coach Will took over. Nobody said it, but everybody thought it.

"There goes our offense," muttered Tom. "Those two score almost all our points."

Sameer pushed up his glasses. "They'll be back. They love basketball. They'll be back," he repeated with a confidence he didn't feel. He shoved his hands in his pockets, nodded and looked around at the guys. Everyone was shaking their heads.

"Face it, man, they're gone. Like, *gone* gone," Vijay said, swinging his badminton racket.

"I rather think Vijay is right," said Coach Will quietly, lifting a pale face to look over at Sameer. He looked almost ill.

He's not a bad guy, thought Sameer. He's odd, but he's not a bad guy. He's nice. He's trying. He's taken on this team last minute, thrown himself into something he knows nothing about, but he's trying to be positive and creative. How would any of us do parachuted into directing one of Shakespeare's plays?

Sameer racked his brain for something to say. He fell back on a few comforting sports clichés.

"Well, then, Coach Will, looks like we'll have to make some adjustments to the lineup, maintain our composure, get back on track and get our heads back into basketball." He looked around. "Right, guys?"

There was a pause, then Vijay said, "Right!" in a hearty, overly loud voice. He shot a nervous glance at Coach Will, who smiled sadly.

"Brave Sameer. Loyal Vijay. What would we do without you?" He turned to look at the rest of the team. "Well, Anil and Rochon spoke very plainly." He took a deep breath and pushed back his hair. He spread his hands wide. "I can only say that I'm terribly sorry if I've caused you to be laughed at or ridiculed by your peers. Sometimes one gets carried away and forgets what it's like to be thirteen or fourteen." His voice fell to a murmur on the last sentence, as if he was talking to himself.

He stood looking at the floor, then sighed. "*What's done can't be undone*," he said. "Oops, sorry—Shakespeare again. I really must work on that. Habit." He jammed his fist against his mouth, biting his thumbnail.

"It's okay," said Nikho. "Doesn't kill us to get a little culture."

There was a little ripple of laughter, a slight loosening of tension.

"Yeah," said Nate. He pointed at Nikho with the racket he still held. "Deekho's right."

Mr. Williams rubbed a hand over his forehead, his face strained. "I suppose I should try to see if Anil and Rochon…I should probably…" He looked young and lost as his voice trailed off. "Sameer, would you possibly…?" He waved his arm vaguely at the gym, meaning "take over all this."

Sameer said, "Sure. Of course."

When Mr. Williams had gone, Vijay said, "Maybe we should just cancel this practice, hey, Sameer?"

"Well, what do you guys think?" asked Sameer. For once, he wasn't sure what to do.

"Yeah, let's cancel," said Tom, tossing down his racket.

"What? Why?" said Kyle. "'Cause Rochon and Anil quit? Forget them. They think this team's all about them."

"Okay, okay, we practice," said Tom, raising his hands in surrender. "But seriously, while Coach Will is gone, don't you guys think Anil and Rochon had a point? Don't you think Coach Will is a bit...weird?"

"Yeah, he's weird. Of *course* he's weird." Nikho rolled his eyes. "Tell us something we *don't* know, Tom."

"But Coach Boss was *bean*," said Nate. They stared at him blankly.

"Mean," stage-whispered Vijay in translation.

"Good point, Nate," said Sameer. "Nobody was threatening to quit the team when Coach Boss was around."

"That's because he'd have killed whoever quit. Or made their lives miserable. Look what happened to Alex."

The team fell silent, remembering how early in the season an injured teammate had brought his parents in to explain to Coach Boss that he was leaving under doctor's orders. Coach Boss had pretended to be supportive and understanding but later harassed Alex mercilessly in class and in the halls for being a "quitter," a "coward" and a "momma's boy." Alex had eventually changed schools.

"We've only got seven players without Anil and Rochon," pointed out Hassan (or Mohammed).

"So what?" said Mohammed (or Hassan), glaring at his brother. "You only need five."

"You need subs. Anyway, they were our only real shooters. The scorers," argued Hassan (or Mohammed).

"Yeah, ball hogs usually get the points," said Mohammed (or Hassan).

"Having only two subs *will* be tough," Sameer felt obliged to point out. "It means a lot of game time, a lot of running, not much rest. And we can't add guys to the team midseason."

"So? We got us, right?" said Nikho. "Anil and Rochon think the team's just going to collapse without them."

"No way."

"Nope."

"Yeah, we're not folding the team just because of them, are we?" said Kyle.

"No, we are not," said Kenneth emphatically in his deep voice.

"I was just gedding into dis fencing thing," said Nate, whiffing his racket in the air. "Only let's switch pardners. Deekho's killing me."

"Move your huge feet, man," laughed Nikho. "If you can lift them."

Sameer straightened his shoulders. "Coach Will was actually right, hey? Footwork. It helps you stay with your man. How about another five minutes doing the fencing thing, and then I've got a new defense drill. Okay?" He clapped his hands loudly. "Let's do this!"

FIFTEEN
That's Gotta Hurt

The rest of the team had gone.

"Well? What do you think?" Sameer asked Vijay.

"I think I'm *starving*," said Vijay.

Sameer dug in his backpack for a granola bar and tossed it to Vijay. "No, I mean about the whole Anil/Rochon thing."

"It is what it is," Vijay said, chewing and shrugging philosophically.

"I thought Coach Will would come back to the practice. Don't you think it's odd that he didn't come back?"

"Whatever. He's probably just, like, worn out from all the drama. Me, I don't mind drama. Makes things interesting. Shakes things up a bit."

Sameer was barely listening to Vijay. He felt uneasy. "Anyway, I'm going to stay for the girls' practice. I was talking to Coach Morrison today, and she's going to be running a few new defense drills that I think we should try."

"I'll stay too," Vijay said quickly. "After all, I *am* the team manager. You might need some specialist managing…manager…ing."

"Riiight. You're all about the team, Vijay. I thought you were starving."

"I'm okay. You got any more food in there?" He grabbed Sameer's backpack.

"Hey." Sameer snatched it back. "How many millions of times have I told you that my stuff is private? Look, I've got a samosa in my locker. It's a day old, but you can have it."

"Okay, I'll go get it." Vijay stood up.

"Uh, you might need me for that," Sameer said.

"Nah, I know your combination. Seven, fifteen, twenty-five, right?"

"Vijay! How do you—no, for your information that is *not* right."

"Okay, look, we'll both go to your locker, and I'll pretend not to know your combination. Feel better? But let's go *quick*. The girls will be here any minute."

They jogged through the empty halls to Sameer's locker, where Sameer shielded his lock with his body as he entered seven, fifteen, twenty-five. As soon as the locker opened, Vijay shouldered Sameer aside, reached down and rummaged on the bottom shelf.

"You usually chuck food down here, which, by the way, isn't very sanitary. Ka-ching! Got it. Thanks, buddy. See you back in the gym."

Sameer slammed his locker shut, turned to follow Vijay, then hesitated. He thought maybe he should go down to the drama room to see if Mr. Williams was there and tell him how the practice went. He waved to Gary, the custodian who was pushing a broom down at the end of the science hall.

The drama room was a dingy, almost-forgotten room at the far end of what was called "the arts hallway." There was an art room across the hall from the drama room, but there hadn't been a drama program for years, so the drama space had been used mostly as a huge storage locker, a dumping ground for books, files or equipment that didn't fit anywhere else in the school.

The door to the drama room was ajar, and the interior was dim. But there was a light on somewhere behind the wall of stacked boxes. Sameer pushed open the door slightly and walked a little ways into the room. He opened his mouth to call Mr. Williams's name and then froze as he heard Mr. Williams's voice. It sounded like he was right beside Sameer.

"I can't. No. Mother. *Mom*. I have play rehearsal at seven." He was talking on the phone, on the other side of the boxes. "No, it's nothing to do with Steve being there." Sameer started to back out of the room, groping behind him to find the door in the gloom. Mr. Williams's voice got louder. "No, Steve's a *prince* of a fellow—when he's not drinking. Sorry...Mom, I'm twenty-five years old. I'm not calling a man I scarcely know *Dad*. Yes, I'm *under your roof* at the moment, but not for long…I *do* have a job…not exactly in theater, no…yes, with *children*. That's what teaching involves…that's my business…Look, I'm sorry…"

Sameer scuttled back into the hall, feeling oddly guilty for hearing as much as he had. He stood there uncertainly for a few seconds, staring at the drama-room door. The murmur of Mr. Williams's voice stopped. The phone call was over.

Should I try again? wondered Sameer. Mr. Williams sure seemed like he could use some cheering up.

"Mr. Williams?" Sameer said, knocking on the door. He knocked louder. No answer.

"Mr. Williams?" Sameer opened the door and walked to the end of the wall of boxes. "Mr. Williams!" *This is ridiculous. I know he's here.*

Sameer peered around the wall of boxes. Mr. Williams was slumped in a fold-up chair at a tiny desk, his head leaning on one hand. He had headphones on, and he was staring out the dark windows.

Sameer waved an arm to attract his attention, and Mr. Williams jumped up, flushing and fumbling awkwardly with his headphones.

"Sorry, Sameer, I was lost in Beethoven. Have you been there long?" he asked quickly.

"No, I just got here," Sameer lied. "Just now. Saw the light on."

"Ah. Well. Come in, come in." Mr. Williams moved some boxes, grabbed another chair and unfolded it with a snap. It slithered on some papers on the floor before Mr. Williams found a bare spot. "Sorry, this room is a bit of a mess." He looked around. "A lot of a mess." He sighed. "Do you know, Sameer, that the stage you can't see because of those recycling bins and that shop equipment is actually raised up a couple of steps? It's an actual stage! And there's actually a rod up there"—he pointed into the dim ceiling—"for a curtain? There is a small theater buried under here somewhere. It would take an army to find it though. But I'm babbling. What can I do for you?"

"I just thought you might be happy to know that everything went fine at practice. The guys wanted to keep slashing away with the fencing drill for a while, and then we worked on defense. Blocking out, switching, following checks, even a press."

"Ah." Mr. Williams sank back down into his chair. "Good, good," he said vaguely. "I did try to talk to Anil and Rochon, but they were unwilling to listen. They were"—he gave Sameer a twisted smile—"rather rude. But then, they're young."

"They're fifteen. No excuse for being rude," said Sameer. "Jerks."

"No, no," Mr. Williams protested, "it's an emotional age."

They sat in silence for a minute.

"Do you find that sometimes things don't turn out the way you imagine they will?" mused Mr. Williams. His voice was sad as he looked off into the distance. "I'm speaking generally, of course, Sameer. You're so young—what could you know of failure or loss?"

Plenty, thought Sameer. A quick memory of his grandmother laughing surfaced in Sameer's mind, and he pushed it away.

"Well," Sameer said, hoping his voice didn't sound strange, "I tried out for the basketball team, but I got cut."

"Really?" Mr. Williams sat up. "I'm very sorry, Sameer. That must have been terribly disappointing. You would have been a loyal, hard-working teammate."

Sameer shrugged.

"*When sorrows come, they come not single spies, but in battalions*," said Mr. Williams.

"Meaning bad things come in bunches?" said Sameer.

"Exactly! You put it well. Take, for instance, the Gladiators basketball team. It all started so well, things were really on track, and now it appears to be falling apart." He held up a hand as Sameer tried to object. "Hear me out, Sameer. Or this school play. I thought it would be such fun, that there would be so much youthful energy and enthusiasm for the play."

"And there's not?" Sameer asked, already sensing the answer.

"Four students have shown up from my school-wide call for auditions. Four. And one of them doesn't even want a role. She only wants to help with costumes. And nobody wants to be the king. Can you believe that? Henry the Fifth, the heroic king!" Mr. Williams brandished an imaginary sword before letting his arm fall.

"Sucks," said Sameer sympathetically. "But maybe Shakespeare is a little—I don't know—complicated? Intimidating?"

"Oh, I did think of that." Mr. Williams leaned forward, his elbows on his knees. "But I've stripped the play down to its barest of bare bones, a mere outline, and translated some of it into more modern language! I'll narrate a voice-over, and the actors only need to memorize a few paragraphs each, just the main speeches. Mrs. Lee's rather dampening advice was to keep it under forty-five minutes." He sat back in his chair, looked out the black window and sighed. "But how I had imagined battle scenes! Pageantry! Ferocity! A *Henry V* that the kids would be proud of!"

Sameer watched Mr. Williams straighten and push his hair behind his ears.

"I'm sorry, Sameer, you don't need to hear me whining about my little troubles. Now, about the basketball. We're down to…how many players?"

"Seven," Sameer said, relieved they were back to a subject he knew something about.

"Seven. And we need…how many?"

"Well, only five play on the court at once. So we've got two subs."

"Not optimal."

"No."

"Be honest with me, Sameer," Mr. Williams said, sitting forward with his hands gripping each other tightly. "Would it be better if we just scrapped the whole thing? I'll be frank. I thought I would help out when Mrs. Lee seemed desperate to find somebody to coach, but I don't feel that I'm at all the right person for the job. I'm not particularly athletic. I know almost nothing about basketball— although I have your binder, I've started watching the games on television, and I've been trying to learn from the girls' very knowledgeable coach. But I still feel a bit of a fraud every time they call me Coach Will."

"Listen, Mr. Williams," said Sameer, "all of the guys in that gym want you to stay. They want to play basketball. Look, sure, you're…you've got a… different way of coaching than most people. But, for example, you hit the nail on the head that we desperately need to work on defense. And you understand *people*. And you're not a screamer. And the guys like you."

Mr. Williams gnawed at his thumbnail, looking unconvinced.

Sameer tried again.

"So it looks like you have a question to ask yourself, Mr. Williams: To be or not to be a basketball coach? I don't know what Shakespeare would've answered there, but he seemed like a pretty adventurous guy. A go-getter, a team player. In sports talk we'd say, 'It ain't over till it's over.' Meaning stick with it, because there's still time for things to improve."

Mr. Williams gave a bark of laughter.

"Sameer, you are a treasure."

"Nah," said Sameer, smiling with pride at the compliment, "just a heck of an assistant coach."

SIXTEEN
King of the Court

The Gladiators lost by sixteen points to St. Paul later that week. On the quiet bus ride back to their school, Sameer pulled out the red binder Coach Will had returned to him. He flipped to the yellow tab where he'd saved a copy of the score sheet from every game that year.

"Guys, listen up! The last time we played St. Paul, we lost by forty-two points. *Forty-two points*! The score was 28–70. Blowout, right? But today? The score was 16–32. Guys, we held *St. Paul* to thirty-two points! They're fourth in the rankings!"

"Their shots weren't falling," said Tom. "Maybe they just had a bad game."

"Or maybe," argued Sameer, "we had a good game! Maybe we *made* their shots not fall."

"Sixteen points isn't exactly lighting up the scoreboard," said Kenneth.

"No, but we scored sixteen without Anil and Rochon. And it was our defense that held them to thirty-two. *That's* why their shots weren't falling! Because we were right on them whenever they got the ball. Nate blocked seven shots! Guys! This was a good game!"

Mr. Williams looked in the rearview mirror. "I have to agree with Sameer," he called back. "I was proud of how hard you boys worked out there. You, ah, dug most deeply and gave 110 percent!"

The guys grinned at each other. Mr. Williams had been doing that all week, awkwardly substituting sports clichés for his usual Shakespearean quotes. When Nate had blocked that last shot, Mr. Williams had jumped to his feet and shouted, "*That* is what *I* am talking about!"

"I'm not sure, but I think I liked him more when he was the goth poet," whispered Vijay.

"Oh, he's still the goth poet," said Sameer.

"Don't be too sure," said Vijay. "Check out the Gladiators sweatshirt he's wearing. And I saw him in the bathroom trying on a ballcap. Imagine that for a minute, Sameer. Coach Will in a ballcap. All that long hair danglin' out the back. Lame. Like, *lame* lame."

Sameer shrugged and went back to trying to decipher Vijay's stats. "Vijay, what is this?"

Vijay groaned. "Oh, *man*. Stats again? You know what, Sameer? I *hate* stats. I hate being manager. I thought it would be all important and impressive, but it's not. Nobody's impressed. Gracie hasn't even mentioned it. It's boring, and you might be surprized to hear this, but I don't think I'm any good at it. It's all 'rebound' this and 'shot attempt' that, and tick the stupid little box. I can't even watch the game!"

"I didn't know you hated it that much."

"Well, I do. Like—"

"Please don't say, 'Like, *hate* hate it.' I got it."

"I miss being the Gladiators' mascot," Vijay said, idly scraping away at the frost on the bus window with his fingernail. "Now *that* was fun. Desmond sucks at it. Did you see him last home game? Wouldn't wear the helmet and stood against the wall texting most of the game. No energy. No enthusiasm. No 'Rrrraaaarrrgh!'" Vijay bared his teeth, shaking his fists above his head. "Gladiator energy, you know?" He dropped his arms by his sides and shook his head sadly.

"You *were* really good at that," Sameer said. "You always had the crowd eating out of your hand. You really got them going."

Vijay turned to him excitedly. "I did, didn't I? It was fun. It was *so* much fun. They loved the Gladiator Chop—you know, the scissor chop with the arms? Everyone went wild with that one. Or Go Bananas, where I chucked bananas into the crowd." Vijay smiled and leaned his head back on the seat. "Ah, there's nothing like it, Sameer. When the crowd's roaring and everyone's looking at you and laughing at what you do...Yeah, I miss the crowd. I miss all that."

"Sounds like you're a born performer," Sameer said, correcting Vijay's muddled addition in the number-of-assists column. Then he stopped, looked at Vijay and grabbed his arm. "Vijay, you're a *performer*!"

"Why are you all creepy-intense all of a sudden? Stop it—you're freaking me out!"

"Vijay, listen," said Sameer slowly, the idea taking shape in his brain. "You would be *perfect* for the lead role in the school play. *Henry V*! You could be Henry V! The king of England!"

"Get out of here." Vijay shoved Sameer's shoulder.

"I'm serious, Vijay."

"Me? An actor?"

"Why *not* you?"

"True. I mean, I do have the face, right? The look, the voice, the presence." Vijay sat up, straightening his skinny shoulders.

"And clearly the ego," said Sameer.

"Why didn't I think of this before? It's so obvious."

"You do love being in front of an audience," said Sameer.

"An audience. Did you say it was the main part?"

"Yeah, it's the king. Henry the Fifth. It's spelled Henry Vee, but *V* is the roman number for five. Anyway, he's Henry the Fifth. That's the title of the play. *Henry V*. The title-lead role."

"The titley-*leader* role…"

"And it's about some battle that Henry leads an army to."

"I do have the gladiator experience for the sword stuff! And the badminton fencing!" pointed out Vijay, sounding excited. "Wait, this Henry Five's not one of those guys that kills people to get to be king, right? I mean, he's a cool guy?"

"I think the play is about him being a hero. That was the impression I got. And it's *fifth*, not *five*. Henry the Fifth."

"A hero…" Vijay stared off into space, his mouth open. "Sameer, I think I'm going to do this thing. You know when you have a feeling in your gut—"

"Yeah, Vijay, you've told me *all* about your gut feelings," said Sameer wearily. "No more gut stuff, please."

"—and your gut says, 'How can you not do this?' And you say to your gut, 'Gut, you're right, it's perfect.' I'm going to do it. I'm definitely going to do it!"

"Well? Tell him." Sameer gestured to Mr. Williams in the driver's seat.

"Oh, yeah, that's my director, right? Um, Coach Will?" called Vijay. Mr. Williams looked into the rearview mirror. "I hear you've got a vacancy for a king? For a king part? A guy called Henry Five?"

"Henry *the Fifth*!" Sameer hissed irritably. "Jeez, Vijay."

"We are looking for a king, yes, Vijay," said Mr. Williams, his eyebrows rising. "Are you saying you might be interested in the role?"

"Yeah. I mean…" Vijay put on a lame English accent. "I am indeed, good sir!"

The guys in the bus laughed.

"Excellent!" Mr. Williams slapped the steering wheel. "I'm delighted, Your Majesty! Rehearsal tonight at 7:00 PM."

Vijay turned an excited face to Sameer.

"Wow, he must know my work, hey? Did you hear that? Hired on the spot! Didn't even need to audition!"

"That's great, Vijay. Great."

"And look, Sameer, about the manager thing—"

"Don't worry about it," said Sameer, clutching the clipboard of useless-squiggle stats to his chest. "There are only a few games left. We'll manage, no pun intended. And after all, you'll have more important things to worry about."

Vijay was digging in his backpack. He pulled out his dollar-store gladiator sword.

"What are you—? You actually carry that around with you, Vijay? Seriously?"

"Yeah, never know when you'll need it. Like now! Time to shake a spear! Get it? Shakespeare?"

"Lame," Sameer said, laughing.

"Yes, Sameer," Vijay said in a loud, theatrical, vaguely English-accented voice, standing in the aisle and brandishing the sword unsteadily as the bus lurched around a corner. "I *will* have more important things to worry about! Like ENGLAND! And VICTORY!"

Sameer shook his head as the whole bus burst into applause.

But he was smiling. And so were Mr. Williams's eyes in the rearview mirror.

SEVENTEEN
Weight Training

"**H**i, Sameer. Hey, Vijay, saw you Shakespearing in the hall yesterday," said Gracie.

"Yeah?" Vijay gulped down a huge mouthful of sandwich. "You saw? Well, Williams saw my gladiator work and said, like, *Vijay, man, only you can do it. We really need you for the lead role.* Henry Five."

"The Fifth," Sameer corrected quietly.

"Yeah, Henry Five, the *Fifth*." Vijay nodded significantly, like it was a sequel. "Lead role. No big deal."

"My friend Kayley's in the play too," said Gracie.

"Oh, yeah, Kayley. She's nice, even though she's only a duke," Vijay said dismissively. Sameer looked away as Vijay launched into a rambling explanation of how the play was really a macho slug fest, even though all the other parts were being played by girls.

"Anyway, it looks kind of fun," said Gracie. "Why are you guys rehearsing in the hall though?"

"Ah, sound quality and space and—"

"Oh yeah, the drama room is a dump," Gracie said, her hands on her hips.

"Possibly, but the hallway really brings Shakespeare to the people, you know."

"Oh brother," said Gracie, rolling her eyes at Sameer and walking away.

Vijay shook Sameer's shoulder. "That was the longest conversation we've ever had! I think she was impressed. Did you think she was impressed?"

"Oh yeah, Vijay. Swooning," said Sameer absently. He was thinking.

"So, Coach Williams is sick today, but we'll be introducing a new component to our practice," announced Sameer at practice. "Weight training."

"What? How?" asked Kyle. "There's no weights. There's no weight room."

"Yeah, Sameer, we going to be lifting each other?"

"I pick Nikho!" yelled Hassan and Mohammed at the same time, dibsing the smallest guy on the team.

"Okay, okay," said Sameer. "Actually, that's not a bad idea. Anyway, we're going to be sort of combining a workout with something that needs to be done around here. Come with me."

He led them out of the gym. The girls' basketball team was just rounding the corner of the hallway. Ms. Morrison, the girls' coach, said, "Oh, good. Sameer. Everybody here?" Sameer nodded. "Great idea, by the way. Let's go."

Mystified, the teams jogged after Ms. Morrison's bobbing ponytail, down the arts hallway to the drama room.

She turned at the door.

"Listen up, teams!" she called over the babble of voices. "This is our weight training! We're clearing the drama room. Poor Mr. Williams has been trying to put together a play in this mess.

He's cleared a little space, but he doesn't know where anything goes. It'll be a nice surprise for him to have it all cleaned up. Should've been done months ago. So let's get in there and work hard! There's, what, twenty of us? Let's see it cleared in an hour. Everything out here, lined against the wall, please. Except any fold-up chairs you find. Stack those against the wall in the drama room."

Ms. Morrison barked further orders like a drill sergeant and had both teams working hard within minutes. The piles of boxes in the hallway grew. Ms. Morrison unlocked the art room and told a group of them to cart in all the old easels, canvases and supplies and stack them neatly in a corner.

"Had to get Mrs. Lee to talk Mrs. Brezinski into taking all her old stuff back into the art room," Ms. Morrison said to Sameer. "Artistic, yes. Cooperative, no."

Gary, the custodian, had wheeled a big recycling bin into the hall, and he and Ms. Morrison went through box after box.

"Seriously, Gary, look at this. A box of exams from 1989!"

Nikho found an ancient boom box with a tape still in it behind the stage. He plugged it in, and '80s music filled the air as both teams worked up a sweat clearing the room.

"Hey," said Vijay with a big smile, awkwardly grooving to the music, "this feels like a party! Gracie," he called across the room, "does it feel like a party to you?"

"Would you *help* already, Vijay?" Gracie snapped, barely looking at him as she and another girl hauled a huge box into the hallway.

"See? Gracie and me, we're talking all the time now," Vijay whispered to Sameer.

"Three overhead projectors." Ms. Morrison shook her head. "I wonder if the museum would want these."

Mr. Williams had been right. A large proper stage, raised three steps off the floor, emerged from the rubble. The stage and the wall behind it had once been painted black but were now a dingy, faded and chipped charcoal.

"Hey, they must really have put on plays here once," said Nikho to Sameer, dragging a long dusty roll of fabric into the hall. He pointed to the tangled hooks clamped to the material. "I think maybe this was the curtain."

"Still a few stage sets back here," called Kenneth, flipping through a pile of old cardboard.

"Better keep any drama-related things," Sameer said. "Mr. Williams might need them."

They started a stash of useful drama stuff at the back of the room: a rolled-up canvas panel painted like a forest, a slab of plywood roughly cut in the shape of a car, three tall stage lamps that might work if the bulbs were changed, some long blue cardboard-cutout waves, a roll of yellow carpet with bricks sharpied on it.

"The Yellow Brick Road!" said Gracie. "I bet they did *The Wizard of Oz*!"

It became a scavenger hunt, with everyone digging and calling out their finds.

"Orange flags! Nine of them! I think they're the ones for the soccer field that Coach Boss freaked out about missing."

"A huge cardboard castle!"

"A big painted mountain!"

"Bucket of Monopoly money!"

"Cardboard horses!"

"A ratty old fur thing." Sameer poked at it with a flagpole, assuring himself that it wasn't a dead animal. "What is it? A rug? A blanket?" Sameer picked it up, shook it out and spread it out wide.

Vijay snatched it from Sameer's hands and draped it around his shoulders like a cape. He walked slowly to the middle of the dusty stage, threw out one arm and quoted his lines in a booming voice to the back of the room:

"*The fewer the men, the greater the share of the glory*! Um…something, something…Oh, I know! *I pray thee, don't wish for one more guy!*"

"Shakespeare said *guy*?" Sameer was skeptical.

"Close enough," Vijay snapped. Then he looked off into the distance again. "*We few, we many few—*"

"*Many few*? That doesn't even make sense."

"Artistic theater types will understand," Vijay said grandly. "You can go back to your little stats, Sameer." He waved his hand dismissively.

"Sounding good, Vijay," said a girl with a box in her hands.

"Hey, thanks, Kayley!" Vijay showed all his teeth in a big smile. "We got a real stage now! Fit for a king, right?"

He hopped off the stage and came over to where Sameer was dragging a big box of books.

"Hear that, Sameer? Did you hear how Kayley said '*Sounding great, Vijay*?'"

"I heard her say *sounding good*," Sameer said. "Look, could you *help* with this?"

"*Sounding great, Vijay*," Vijay repeated, slumping down with a sigh to sit on the box Sameer was trying to pull. "Kayley," he said. "Isn't that a cool name? I don't know if you noticed, but she's got huge eyes, and she's really funny."

Sameer looked at Vijay. "And you really *like* like *her* now? Seriously, Vijay? What about Gracie?"

Vijay nodded sadly. "Yeah, she might take it hard. I think she was really into me. I mean, she hid it well, but still." He looked over at Kayley, who was laughing with a friend. "I don't want to hurt anybody, Sameer, but you gotta be honest, right? Like, *honest* honest with yourself. Listen to your gut, right? I don't think it would've worked with me and Gracie. But Kayley…"

Sameer leaned against the box and let Vijay talk.

He looked over to where Gracie was pushing a box with some other girls. They were laughing and arguing. Vijay glanced at Gracie too.

"You think she'll be okay?" Vijay asked anxiously.

"I think she'll get over it, Vijay."

EIGHTEEN
Wild Card

"I can't thank you enough, Gladiators, for giving new life to the Gladys Spinoza school theater!" Mr. Williams had his hand over his heart at practice the next day. "You are all, ah, major dudes!" The team looked at the floor, trying not to smile. "It was such a wonderful surprise to come back from two *wretched* days with the flu to see the drama room restored to its original glory. *All the world's a stage*, of course, but it's nice to have a *real* one right here in the school."

They did the badminton-fencing drill for footwork, and Sameer had them run piggyback races for strength, alternating teams so nobody could hog Nikho. They were just finishing up the end-of-practice scrimmage when Ms. Morrison appeared at the gym door.

"Hey, Aubry, can I talk to you for a sec?" she called.

Mr. Williams's face lit up. "Absolutely, Agnes! Delighted! Be right there!"

"Agnes?" said Sameer.

Mr. Williams, flustered, gathered his papers and smiled. "*A rose by any other name would smell as sweet.*" He jogged to the door. He and Ms. Morrison talked animatedly before he wrenched open the gym door and held it for her as they left the gym.

Mr. Williams returned five minutes later and called the boys to gather around.

"Oh, Gladiators, some wonderful, wonderful news! As you know, the next game would, sadly, have been our last but for something called, rather fancifully, a wild-card draw. Ah, Sameer, would you explain?"

Sameer nodded. "The top six teams in the league based on wins and points scored go to the playoffs. Like our girls' team. But they also do a wild-card draw for two teams to get into the playoffs, and their record doesn't matter. It's like a lottery, where you win a spot in the playoffs."

Sameer's heart was racing. How could he have forgotten about the wild-card spots? Could they possibly be heading to the playoffs for the first time in Gladiators history?

"Agn—Ms. Morrison has just informed me that the Gladiators boys' team has been selected as a wild-card entry into the playoffs!" Mr. Williams looked around excitedly. "We even get to play the game here, in this very gymnasium, so home-turf advantage!" He gently punched his fist in the air. Mr. Williams's enthusiasm was infectious, and there was excited murmuring among the boys.

"So, who do we play?" asked Tom finally.

"Ah, we are playing against a team called"— Mr. Williams shuffled some papers he was holding—"McGee. Alexander McGee."

There was a dead silence. Sameer's heart sank.

"Is there a problem?" Mr. Williams said uncertainly, looking around at the faces in front of him.

"No problem. Other than that we're going to get *slaughtered*. In *public*," said Kyle.

"McGee's first place in the standings by a long shot," explained Sameer in an aside to Mr. Williams. "They always are. Nobody wants to play them. They hammer everybody." Hassan and Mohammed stood silently, their arms wrapped around their stomachs.

"This was the last team we played before Coach Boss got fired, right?" asked Hassan (or Mohammed).

"Yeah," said Sameer.

"This is not good," said Mohammed (or Hassan). They both shook their heads.

"Great, just great," Tom said. "They'll murder us here, in front of the whole school. Can we back out of this wild-card thing? Can we give the card back? Or give it to some other school?"

"Maybe McGee has some injuries," suggested Nikho. "Anybody know? Like, their big guy. Maybe he's got bad knees?"

"Or their three-point shooter? Number 11? Maybe he's injured his wrist from draining all those threes." Kenneth warmed to the theme.

"Don't be pathetic, guys," said Kyle.

Mr. Williams gnawed on his thumbnail and looked over at Sameer. Sameer took a big breath.

"Look, guys, we've improved a lot since we last played McGee," he said, holding his hand up to silence the team's protests. "We have. I have proof right here!" He tapped his red binder. "Is it going to be a tough game? Absolutely. Will we have to work harder than we've ever worked before? You bet. But if we can come up with a strategy to contain them offensively, shut down their points, I think we have a chance."

"A chance to *win*?" said Tom in disbelief.

"No, a chance to not be humiliated," said Nikho.

"So anyway, last league game is on Tuesday," Sameer said in a brisk, practical voice. "When's the playoff game, Coach?"

"Thursday, I believe." He checked the paper. "Yes, Thursday. Gosh, only two days before the play performance!"

Thursday, thought Sameer, his hands starting to sweat. They only had five days.

He nodded, his face impassive. "Good. We've got five whole days."

NINETEEN
Never Say Die

It was the last home game of the season in the Gladiators gym, the wild-card game.

Being a coach instead of an announcer is a whole lot less fun, thought Sameer. The noise in the gym was so loud, Sameer could feel it rumbling up through the bench where he and Mr. Williams sat, tensely watching the clock tick away the ten minutes to the start of the game. If he'd been calling the game, he'd have loved the atmosphere in the gym. He would have smiled the whole time. As it was, his jumpy nerves could have used a little less noise.

"Where are they?" he said for the fifth time. "Hassan and Mohammed are never late." He checked his phone. No texts.

Mr. Williams sat with his elbows on his knees, watching the five Gladiators warm up.

"It's the atmosphere of an opening-night performance," he said, "only much, much louder." He bit his thumbnail.

"They'll be here," Sameer said, trying to reassure himself as much as Mr. Williams. "They'll be here." He rubbed his hands together. They felt like ice.

Mrs. Lee bustled over to where they sat. Her face was worried. "Only five players? What's up?" She looked from Sameer to Mr. Williams, then sensed it wasn't the time for talking. "I'll see if we have any snacks or Gatorade in the staff room for halftime. Good luck!" She trotted away, heels clicking and black hair bobbing. Sameer saw her stop and talk with a group of parents. Nate's mom, Nikho's dad, a tall man he didn't know and—wait— his own mother and Vijay's mom. Vijay's mom caught his eye, waved and smiled a Vijay smile, lots of big teeth and gums. Sameer waved back, feeling sick to his stomach.

The five remaining Gladiators were trying to do a layup drill, sneaking glances at their opponents, a squad of twelve who were doing a slick three-point-shooting drill.

"Hey, Sameer." Nikho ran over. "Looks like their star shooter *is* injured!"

Sameer looked over at the other bench. Sure enough, number 11 was still in his sweats, just watching the others warm up. Sameer gave Nikho a nervous thumbs-up.

"Where are they?" Sameer muttered, willing Hassan and Mohammed to appear at the gym door.

"Neither of them looked very well in practice yesterday," murmured Mr. Williams. "I hope they don't have that stomach flu that's going around."

"Yeah, well, sometimes you have to play through the pain," snapped Sameer. "Michael Jordan once—"

"Sameer," Mr. Williams said, holding up a conciliatory hand, "you know they'd be here if they could be."

Like they were following a cue, they both gnawed their thumbnails.

Vijay was in full theatrical mode. He was wearing his gladiator costume, but he'd added the dusty fun-fur cape they'd found in the drama room. He "rode in" to blaring music, waving a flag and riding a prop horse, the cardboard bumping awkwardly against his legs. He trotted a figure eight in front of the crowd, rearing back dramatically. Then he fought his way off the horse, propped it against the wall and started organizing the cheering crowd. He had them Glad-I-Ating and thundering their feet against the bleachers in no time.

Gracie, sitting at the scorers' table with Desmond, checked her phone and waved urgently at Sameer. He ran over to her.

"Got a text from Simone, who's coming in to watch the game. She says Hassan and Mohammed's mom dropped them off, but one of them, she's not sure which, threw up on the school steps as he was running in! Their mom made them both get back in the van, and they left!"

Sameer and Gracie looked at each other, a wave of mutual fear washing over them.

"So you got five players," Gracie said in a panic. "Five guys, Sameer, to play *McGee*!"

Sameer straightened. "We got five. All you need to play a basketball game. Have fun calling the game, Gracie."

Gracie looked at him with renewed respect. "You rock, Sameer! Good luck!"

We're going to need all the luck we can get, Sameer thought, wiping his clammy hands on the sides of his pants.

The two-minute warning buzzer went off.

"Hey, Sameer." Vijay ran over. "Somebody just told me that Hassan and Mohammed puked all over the school steps. They're sick." Under his ridiculous bobble-head helmet, Vijay's face looked worried. "Did you hear me, man? They're not coming!"

"Yeah, I already know. Thanks. Look, we're going to need the crowd to be our sixth man, okay? Energy, enthusiasm, sheer *noise*. Gladiate your heart out this game, Vijay."

"Absolutely. I'll give it everything I got!" Vijay hovered near the bench, swinging his sword, watching the McGee team huddle up. "I'll just wish the guys good luck before the game starts, and then, oh man, I'm gonna get this place rocking."

Sameer slapped hands with the guys coming back to the bench, then turned and whispered to Mr. Williams, "Hassan and Mohammed are sick."

Mr. Williams nodded. He was surprisingly calm. "Boys, boys, huddle up," he said.

"Where are Hassan and Mohammed, Coach?" asked Tom, panic making his voice higher. "The game's starting! Aren't they coming?"

Mr. Williams hesitated. Sameer, with an eye on the clock, jumped in. "They're sick," he said, "so this is the team. The five of you. Five's all we need to play a game."

"What? The five of us? You must be joking. Are you *kidding*?" said Tom.

"Does he look like he's kidding? I think it's time to shut up now, Tom," said Nate.

Sameer took a deep breath. "Okay, guys, listen up."

The team, Vijay and Mr. Williams circled around Sameer, looming over him. He looked around at them. They looked worried, nervous, afraid. He looked at his friends, guys he'd known since they were all in first grade, using their whole bodies to huck up balls nowhere near the baskets.

"Guys, it's time to dig in and dig deep. *Deep.* We've practiced for five days straight, and now it's time to give it all you got. Give this game everything. Sure we're outnumbered. But this is when character counts, and there's a lot of character and a lot of heart on this team. Think back and remember why you wanted to play on this team. Remember playing in the gym at lunch? After school? Remember bribing Gary with donuts to let us use the gym in the summer?" The guys nodded, smiling nervously. They remembered. "*That's* how we're going to go out and play. In *our* gym, in *our* school. Just a bunch of guys who LOVE THIS GAME!" shouted Sameer.

Mr. Williams smiled. "I couldn't have said it better myself."

"But Sameer," interrupted Tom, "we have five players! *Five.* They're going to run us into the ground. We have no subs. Not one sub! If we only had one more guy..."

"Hey!" said Vijay excitedly. "It's just like the battle in my play!"

Mr. Williams stared at Vijay. "Why, you're right, Vijay!"

"Guys," Vijay said urgently, "it's like Henry Five! Listen. England—like, you guys—is hugely outnumbered by France—McGee—in this battle, and the English are all like, 'Oh man, this sucks! If only we had a few more guys!' and King Henry— that's me—does his big speech, inspiring them to fight."

"So inspire us, Vijay," said Nikho. "Now."

The buzzer went off.

"Gotta be quick, here, Vijay," Sameer said, putting his arm around his friend's shoulders.

Vijay closed his eyes for a second. His thin face was serious as he recited, "*The fewer men, the greater share of honour. God's will! I pray thee, wish not one man more…From this day to the ending of the world, we shall be remembered.*" He looked around the circle, and shouted above the roar of the crowd, "*We few, we happy few, we band of brothers!*"

Mr. Williams raised his head from the huddle and turned his face to the wall, blinking hard.

"Nice, Vijay," whispered Sameer, patting him on the back.

"Let's do this!" cried Nate, shaking the circle.

"Yeah, let's do this," screamed Nikho.

Kenneth, Tom and Kyle nodded.

"'Band of brothers' on three."

Everyone put an arm into the circle.

"One, two, three, BAND OF BROTHERS," the Gladiators roared at the top of their lungs and ran out onto the court.

TWENTY
Take It to the Hoop

"**A**nd big Nate comes up with another monster block!" shouted Gracie into the microphone, her voice barely audible over the pounding noise of the crowd. "Hey, you guys are making me lose my voice here!"

Vijay was madly orchestrating the Stamp and Scream for Your Gladiator Team cheer.

"That's at least ten blocked shots for Nate! What are they feeding these guys? They've been total *beasts* on defense!"

The Gladiators had started out badly, giving up a quick ten points and racking up four fouls.

Just as Sameer jumped to his feet, Mr. Williams called a time-out.

"Yeah, good, time-out. I was just going to do that," Sameer babbled. He was frantically trying to think of something to say to the team when Nate blurted out, "It's nice not to get screamed at in time-outs. I used to hate them."

"Oh dear," said Mr. Williams. "That sounds dreadfully counter-productive. Ah, no, no screaming. We have established that I am not a screamer. To be honest, I see a group of boys who only need to calm down and believe in themselves. Relax. Breathe. As Shakespeare says, *All things are ready, if our minds be so.*"

"Freaky," Kyle said with a shake of his head. "I think I'm actually starting to understand that guy."

"Excellent!" Mr. Williams laughed as the ref blew the whistle. "Well, then, here's another. *Once more unto the breach!* Meaning get in there, Gladiators, and play *your* game!"

"Nice." Sameer nodded at Mr. Williams, who smiled and shrugged.

"I have my moments."

The Gladiators seemed more settled, and, unexpectedly, they started scoring. Nikho was tireless on the quick steal and the fast break, Tom scored a few midrange jump shots, and Kyle and Kenneth rebounded like crazy. Nate, his long arms flailing, concentrated on being a wall on defense, using his fencing footwork to stay with his man and help out across the key.

At halftime, the score was 24–12 for McGee. The guys sprawled on the bench. They were silent, red-faced and exhausted, chewing granola bars and taking turns gulping the two Gatorades that Mrs. Lee brought over.

"Hear that?" Sameer asked his team, pointing to the other bench. "Do you hear McGee's coach screaming at them?" The sound was music to Sameer's ears. "It means we're getting under their skin, guys!"

Vijay improvised wildly with some of the drama-room props in the Loud and Proud cheer, and at the buzzer ending halftime he had worked the crowd to a pounding, deafening fever pitch.

In the second half, McGee's coach focused on using the Gladiators' lack of numbers against them, running the ball whenever possible, giving the Gladiators no break.

"Run it, run it!" he screamed at one of his players who'd turned his ankle and was limping and grimacing in pain. "RUN IT, Jackson!"

"But the boy is hurt! That fellow," Mr. Williams said angrily to Sameer, pointing a shaking finger at McGee's coach, "is not a gentleman."

Sameer grinned at him. "A gentleman? No, Coach Will, he's definitely not."

The Gladiators were finding their rhythm, closing down on defense and doggedly sticking to their men. Kyle and Kenneth had agreed at halftime to compete for most rebounds, a contest sharpened by Mr. Williams, who said, "Excellent! Ten dollars to the winner! Oh dear, I probably shouldn't have said that!" Kenneth and Kyle, or K 'n' K, as Gracie had started calling them as she announced the game, were first to every loose ball.

McGee was getting rattled, Sameer realized. The telltale signs were all there—the forced shots, the dumb fouls, the wild passing, the players bickering with each other, the nervous glances over at their coach. It's the worst I've ever seen McGee play, he marveled. Are we really doing this?

It was the last half of the fourth quarter when Kyle grabbed an offensive rebound and put it back up and into the basket. McGee's coach quickly called a time-out. Clearly, he needed to have his team a little closer to scream at them properly, even though they were still up by ten points. The score was 35–25.

Sameer body-slammed the guys as they ran back to the bench.

"Yes, yes!" he screamed, his throat raw. "You guys *rock*!"

The cheer team ran onto the court, covering their ears against the noise in the gym.

In the huddle, Sameer shouted with what was left of his voice, "Just relax now, guys. This is just any other game. We've proved we can keep up with McGee! We've proved that the Gladiators are almost as good as the best team in the league, with five guys, no subs!"

"Yes, boys," said Mr. Williams, patting backs. "Relax. You've proved a lot. A few of you have four fouls. Don't kill yourself these last two minutes. Take it easy."

"Forget that," said Kyle. He stood up and looked at the scoreboard. His face was brick red, his dark hair soaking wet. "Ten points. Let's try to win this."

Kenneth got up, nodding.

Nate looked up with a tired, pale face and grinned. "Sure. Nothing to lose."

"Yeah," screamed Nikho, hauling Tom to his feet. "Let's give it all we got! Throw everything at them! Everything!"

"All right." Mr. Williams laughed, shaking his head. "Go out and kill yourselves these last few minutes, gladiator style!"

I don't even care what happens now, Sameer thought, trying to convince himself as he paced behind the bench. *We've played the game of our lives.* He caught his mother's eye across the court, and she smiled at him as she clapped. *Nani would have been so proud of us. I'm so proud of us.*

Nikho, fast as a hummingbird, pressed the McGee guard on the inbound and managed to steal the ball. A quick layup, and McGee's lead shrank to eight points. Galvanized, the team swarmed all over the McGee squad on defense, forcing them to take a shot that clanged short on the rim. Kyle rebounded and flipped it to Nikho, who dribbled the length of the court and fed Nate, who lumbered in for another quick basket, getting fouled on the shot. Six-point difference, and Nate drained the foul shot. Now a five-point spread.

The score was 35–30.

"Run it! Run it!" the McGee coach screamed as the other team scrambled to fast-break.

The crowd grew silent as the last minute ticked away. Everyone was standing, most of them with their hands against their mouths.

"Twenty-four seconds! The clock is draining down," said Gracie into the mic, her voice hushed. "McGee has to shoot...BLOCKED by Nate!...a scramble for the ball...McGee gets it, no, Kyle snatches it back...eight seconds...Kyle's shot is blocked...he gets his own rebound, swings it around to Nikho...Nikho to Tom...back to Kyle..." Gracie's voice was rising as the crowd chanted down the last seconds of the game "Kyle—oh my!—he alley-oops to Kenneth!"

Sameer stood with his mouth open and his eyes wide as he watched the ball arc through the air toward the hoop. He'd seen Kyle and Kenneth goof around in practice with this pass, but it had never worked, and he never dreamed they would use it in a game. Especially against McGee.

"Kenneth jumps freakishly higher than I've ever—AAAAAAHHH!" screamed Gracie, jumping to her feet at the buzzer. "Slam dunk! He dunks it! On the buzzer! No *way*! I've never seen anybody dunk in junior high!"

The crowd surged onto the court. Sameer saw Mrs. Lee, glasses askew, thumping a grinning Kenneth on the back. Nate's blotchy younger sister had him in a bear hug. Vijay had jumped, screaming, onto Tom's back. A flushed Coach Williams was high-fiving Kyle, and Nikho was jumping wildly all over the place. Gracie stood, fists raised in the Gladiators salute, *whoo-hooing* into the mic.

"Wait, we won, didn't we?" Sameer heard a confused McGee player yell to their coach as they fled the gym.

"Yeah, we won. Barely." The coach shook his head, looking back at the crowd. "Crazy kids don't seem to realize they *lost*."

It doesn't feel like we lost, thought Sameer as he ran over to the guys, getting jostled and shaken and high-fived and hugged.

Losing by three to first-place McGee! McGee, which dominated the league year after year after year. Almost, *almost* knocking McGee out of the playoffs didn't feel like defeat.

It felt like victory.

TWENTY-ONE
Play On

On the intercom the next morning, Mrs. Lee's voice was hoarse. The announcements were punctuated by throat clearing and tea sipping.

"Huge congratulations to the boys' basketball team on a wonderful, thrilling end to the season! A heroic fight by Nate, Kenneth, Kyle, Tom and Nikho, who gave 110 percent, barely falling to McGee in a 35–32 epic battle! Special thanks to Coach Williams, Sameer, Vijay, Gracie, Desmond and the cheer squad. Next week we'll bring the same gladiator spirit to cheer on the girls in their playoff bid. And finally, a reminder that the Dramatic Society's performance of *Henry V* is tomorrow night at 7:00 PM in the drama-room theater. Everyone is welcome."

The school was quiet. Everyone seemed drained and subdued from the frantic excitement of the previous night's game. Everyone except Mr. Williams, who seemed energized. He hummed as he, Sameer and Vijay set out fold-up chairs to accommodate the audience of twenty or so parents and siblings expected for the performance.

Afterward Vijay dumped a box on top of another box by Sameer's locker.

"That's what I got," he whispered, his hand at his throat.

"Wow, a whole box of them!" Sameer said, riffling through the contents. "Vijay, this is great! Why do you have a whole box?"

"Mom. She clears out the dollar stores. I bust one a game," Vijay croaked.

Sameer looked anxiously at Vijay. Sameer's own voice was hoarse, and he hadn't been a screaming-maniac gladiator for an hour and a half.

"Look, just rest your voice, Vijay. The play's tomorrow night. Don't talk all day. And I'm not just saying that to get a break from your yakking, okay?"

"Funny," Vijay croaked.

"*Psssht!* No talking." Sameer rummaged in his backpack and found half a package of lemon lozenges from a long-ago sore throat. "Here, take these."

"Nah, there are some cherry ones here somewhere." Vijay groped at the back of the bottom shelf in Sameer's locker. "Got 'em. So, everything still on?" he said in a strangled whisper.

"Shhh, shhh," soothed Sameer. "Save the voice. You're the only King Henry we've got. Yeah, just finalizing numbers and stuff. Don't worry. It'll be *great*. Go get some hot chocolate or something."

When Vijay had gone, Sameer pulled the boxes into the supply closet around the corner.

Then he went to find Elton, who played trumpet in the band.

"We need a *brrr-brrr-bRRR!*" Sameer explained. "*Really* loud. We thought of taping it, but it'd be way more realistic live."

"That's it? That's all you need? Then I'm gone?"

"In and out in five minutes."

"What do I get for it?" Elton asked, crossing his arms.

Sameer remembered that he had never liked Elton very much. "You get the satisfaction of helping out your school."

"Big deal."

"You'd also be helping out your *friends*," Sameer tried halfheartedly. Elton gave him a long, cold stare.

"Nice, Elton. Five bucks. I'll give you five bucks. A buck a minute."

"Done."

On Saturday night, after a last-minute flurry of activity, the performance was finally under way. There hadn't been enough chairs for the audience streaming in, and Sameer had helped haul more in from the gym. The actors had done an in-costume Friday-afternoon tour of the classrooms to drum up interest in the play, and it had apparently worked. Vijay, resplendent in a gold smock, crown and fun-fur cape, smiled, nodded, looked heroic and did small royalty waves. He saved his voice by letting the others do the talking. His uncharacter-istic silence had intrigued everyone.

And now the drama room was dim and quiet. The curtain was dragged open, a spot-light snapped on, and the play began. Sameer stood in the hallway, waiting for the others. Why am I nervous? he wondered. It's not me onstage in there. He felt a grudging respect for Vijay, whose voice, thankfully, had recovered enough to go on.

Sameer heard the rumble of Mr. Williams's voice narrating the opening of the play, and scuff-ling sounds as the actors moved around on the stage. The audience in the big drama room was silent as the story unfolded. Sameer checked his watch nervously. Twenty minutes to go.

The boys' and girls' basketball teams arrived down the hallway at the arranged time, stifling giggles and whispering. Sameer put his finger to his lips and pointed to the open boxes on the floor. Everyone slipped on net practice jerseys, which only seemed to come in size extra large, and pulled on duct-tape headbands and arm bracelets.

Elton came down the hall, carrying a long black box.

"Hey, what—" he began in a normal voice before being *shhh*ed by everybody. Sameer grabbed his arm and pointed to the stage door.

"What are you guys supposed to be? Freaks? Goths?" whispered Elton.

"Yeah, that's right, Elton. Freakish goths," whispered Sameer wearily. Then he checked his watch and turned to the rest of the people in the hall. "Everybody clear on what we're doing? Good. Elton, when we hear Vijay yell, 'For England!'—should be in about five minutes—that's your trumpet cue. *Loud.* Got it?"

"Hey, Sameer," whispered Gracie, pointing with her sword. "What are those?"

Sameer hesitated. He looked over at the "banners" that he and Vijay had made by duct-taping two of Sameer's grandmother's vivid saris to two flagpoles. Nani had loved color, especially in clothing, and the long swaths of material they had chosen were two of her brightest—a brilliant red and gold, and a deep blue and purple.

Sameer's mother had laughed. *Of course you can use them! I can just hear your nani cackling at the idea! She'd have loved it.*

It had seemed a good idea at the time, but now Sameer wasn't so sure. The banners looked slightly homemade.

"Well, we thought the two leaders could carry them. That's how they used to do it. You know, team colors. We don't have to use them," he said quickly.

"They're gorgeous! Of course we use them. Sameer, you and I take this one, and Kyle and Simone, you take that one. Go! We better get to our positions."

The teams waited. Elton had his trumpet ready. Sameer opened the stage door a crack, listening, listening…

His heart thumped and his hands were sweaty. His ears strained to hear the play. The minutes ticked away, everyone in a clench of anticipation. Sameer heard Vijay give his *We few, we happy few, we band of brothers* speech, and the audience gave a round of enthusiastic applause.

Soon, Sameer thought, coiled and tense.

"For England!" Vijay screamed in a strangled voice, with a quick glance over to the stage door.

Elton's trumpet was so loud it made everyone in the hall jump. He performed a complicated call to battle, not just the three notes Sameer and he had arranged.

"CHAAAAAARRRRRGGGGE!" both teams screamed.

Sameer and Gracie held the sari-banner high as tiny Team England swarmed onto the stage behind a grinning King Vijay, and a way bigger Team France roared into the room from the back and up the aisles. The audience startled, shrieked and then clapped as a ferocious plastic-sword battle ensued onstage and in the aisles. Mr. Williams, who had flinched at the loud and unexpected entrance of the teams, clapped and laughed delightedly, his face alight with surprise and wonder.

It was an epic battle, and under the stage lighting, the net practice jerseys looked close enough to chain armor, and the duct-taped headbands and bracelets looked convincingly military. Team France, both girls and boys, duly fell as arranged, one by one. Sameer dispatched Tom, and Gracie slew Nikho, who died a very gargly, twitchy death. Finally, Kyle allowed Vijay to chase him heroically up and down the aisles and at last collapsed at center stage with a loud thump, the last of the French soldiers to fall at the Battle of Agincourt.

"That was great! Awesome!" said Sameer to Vijay. The battle, the audience's standing ovation, Mr. Williams's emotional speech of thanks—Sameer couldn't believe how well it had all gone.

They walked down the long hallway. Sameer had his nani's battle saris draped over the box of practice jerseys. Vijay was lugging his big box of plastic swords. He was still wearing his crown.

"Yeah, I was pretty spectacular," Vijay admitted, his voice hoarse again.

"I meant the whole thing. The play, the battle, everything."

"Kayley said I was amazing. And Williams said I was a natural. Did you hear how the audience clapped loudest for me? When I came back on? You gotta love that kind of appreciation."

Sameer choked back a cutting remark and said, "You did a great job, Vijay."

"Hey, you guys did a pretty good job too, coming on for the battle scene!" said Vijay. "It was so much better than me pretending to fight imaginary people and stupidly looking off into the distance like I was supposed to do. It really came to life with all you guys!"

"Yeah, it did, didn't it?"

"And Nate crashing into that row of people just made it more realistic somehow."

"Yeah. Nobody got hurt anyway. No blood."

"You know that Williams is going to rope all you guys in for the next play, right?" Vijay said. "I mean, not for the lead role, obviously, but for all the little ones. The crowd scenes."

"Yeah, probably," said Sameer. Somehow, the thought didn't worry him.

Vijay sighed happily. "Man, it's been a great few days, hey? First the game, then the play? But now I'm exhausted. Totally gladiated out. I can barely even carry this box."

"Well, I'm not carrying it, Your Highness, so suck it up."

"Why do we have to haul this stuff all the way to your locker anyway?"

"The practice jerseys have to go to the gym."

"Oh, *man*, that's even farther than your locker! I'm so hungry. Starving. Like, *starving* starving."

"The rest of this is our stuff, Vijay. We can't just dump it anywhere or leave it for Mr. Williams to deal with. And I'm hungry too. Maybe, if you ever take off that stupid crown, we could convince our moms to go get burgers."

"Yes to the burgers, but the crown stays on." Vijay lifted his head regally.

"You're going to wear that thing all month, aren't you?"

"One doesn't stop kinging just because the play ends, my good Sameer."

"Okay, drop it."

"Jealous?" Vijay grinned and thumped his box against Sameer's. "Don't blame you. I would be if *you* looked this good."

"Look, I won't say another word about that stupid crown, but *you* have to listen to my plans for next year's team."

"What? Next year's team? *Now*?"

"Because this was just the beginning, Vijay. These guys showed that they're a special group. One in a million. Actually, five in a million. Seven, counting Hassan and Mohammed."

"Uh-huh. Can you just walk a little quicker there, pal?"

"And next year, we'll be heading to the play-offs again. And not as a wild-card draw. *And* I've figured out that defense really is the key."

"Absolutely," Vijay agreed. "You done? Can we talk burgers now?" He dumped his box in front of Sameer's locker with a big sigh. "Let's just leave these here and go get some *food*."

Sameer dumped his box on top of Vijay's. "We can't just leave them here," he said. "They're blocking, like, three lockers. And Gary might have to clean the halls. We should put the stuff awa—"

"Sameer!"

"Okay, okay." Sameer held up his hand. He was hungry and exhausted. Maybe not every little battle needed to be fought. "Vijay, I can't believe I'm saying this, but you're right. The boxes can wait until morning. Let's just go get some burgers. I feel like we deserve them."

Acknowledgments

Somehow my editor, Sarah "New Nana" Harvey, just keeps getting better at what she does. Thanks to M. and Jen, whose interest in and enthusiasm for each book mean so much to me. Thanks also to all the wonderful players and coaches I've known over the years—children and adults, relatives and friends—too many to name or list. Little bits of you and your game have probably worked their way into this book. Finally, thanks to Hank and Joanne Reinbold for making basketball profound and Shakespeare fun all those years ago.

ALISON HUGHES writes for children of all ages, and her books have been nominated for many awards. Shakespeare had a starring role in her degree in English literature. When she's not writing, she presents at schools, volunteers with family literacy, bikes in the river valley and watches school basketball. She lives with her family in Edmonton. For more information, please visit www.alisonhughesbooks.com.